Heirs to an Empire

Succession, Secrets and Scandal

Following the death of their father, English aristocrat Cedric Pemberton, it's time for the Pemberton heirs to stake their claim in the family empire.

From fashion and cosmetics to jewelry and fragrance, Aurora Inc. is a multinational company, with headquarters all over the world.

As the siblings take the lead in different divisions of the business, they'll face challenges, uncover secrets and learn to start listening to their hearts...

Gabi and Will's Story
Scandal and the Runaway Bride

Charlotte and Jacob's Story
The Heiress's Pregnancy Surprise

Arabella and Burke's Story
Wedding Reunion with the Best Man

Christophe and Sophie's Story
Mistletoe Kiss with the Millionaire

Anemone and Phillipe's Story
A Proposal in Provence

Available now!

Dear Reader,

When I was planning the Aurora series, I somehow knew that there would be one story line that would shake up the Pemberton family. In *A Proposal in Provence*, we meet Anemone Jones— Cedric Pemberton's secret illegitimate daughter. As you can imagine, the Pemberton family is shaken by this news and naturally suspicious of Anemone's motives.

But there's one person who has faith in her: her boss, Phillipe Leroux. And sometimes all you need is one person to believe in you to make everything turn out right.

I hope you enjoy this penultimate story in the Heirs to an Empire series! And stay tuned for an announcement of the last book, where Stephen, the Earl of Chatsworth, finally gets his own happy ending.

Best wishes,

Donna

A Proposal in Provence

Donna Alward

HARLEQUIN

Romance

If you purchased this book without a cover you should be aware that this book is stolen property. It was reported as "unsold and destroyed" to the publisher, and neither the author nor the publisher has received any payment for this "stripped book."

HARLEQUIN®

Romance™

PLEASE RECYCLE
THIS PRODUCT IS RECYCLABLE

Recycling programs
for this product may
not exist in your area.

ISBN-13: 978-1-335-40696-5

A Proposal in Provence

Copyright © 2022 by Donna Alward

All rights reserved. No part of this book may be used or reproduced in any manner whatsoever without written permission except in the case of brief quotations embodied in critical articles and reviews.

This is a work of fiction. Names, characters, places and incidents are either the product of the author's imagination or are used fictitiously. Any resemblance to actual persons, living or dead, businesses, companies, events or locales is entirely coincidental.

This edition published by arrangement with Harlequin Books S.A.

For questions and comments about the quality of this book, please contact us at CustomerService@Harlequin.com.

Harlequin Enterprises ULC
22 Adelaide St. West, 41st Floor
Toronto, Ontario M5H 4E3, Canada
www.Harlequin.com

Printed in U.S.A.

Donna Alward lives on Canada's east coast with her family, which includes a husband, a couple of kids, a senior dog and two zany cats. Her heartwarming stories of love, hope and homecoming have been translated into several languages, hit bestseller lists and won awards, but her favorite thing is hearing from readers! When she's not writing, she enjoys reading—of course!—knitting, gardening, cooking...and she's a *Masterpiece* addict. You can visit her on the web at donnaalward.com and join her mailing list at donnaalward.com/newsletter.

Books by Donna Alward

South Shore Billionaires

Christmas Baby for the Billionaire
Beauty and the Brooding Billionaire
The Billionaire's Island Bride

Heirs to an Empire

Scandal and the Runaway Bride
The Heiress's Pregnancy Surprise
Wedding Reunion with the Best Man
Mistletoe Kiss with the Millionaire

Visit the Author Profile page
at Harlequin.com for more titles.

To all the writers who kept writing during this pandemic. The world is brighter because of you.

PROLOGUE

February

STEPHEN PEMBERTON, EARL OF CHATSWORTH, paced in front of the antique mahogany desk in his office at Chatsworth Manor.

"What are you telling me, George?" He stopped pacing and squared up to face the accountant he'd hired to audit the estate financials. "Where did it go?"

The "it" he was referring to was a sum of money that had been withdrawn biannually from the estate funds for twenty-six years. Not a huge amount compared with the equity in the estate; it amounted to about thirty thousand pounds annually. But over twenty-six years it was more than three-quarters of a million pounds.

"I can try to trace it if you want. Honestly, Lord Pemberton, it's the only anomaly I've found in the audit. That's good news."

Stephen supposed he should be grateful for that. Inheriting the title and the estate at such an early age had been a shock. And the family certainly wasn't hurting for money; Aurora Inc. was massively successful. But Stephen alone was responsible for the estate and his father's legacy. It had been a few years now and the ground seemed to have settled within the family. Performing an audit was, in his opinion, the responsible thing to do.

"Call me Stephen," he said quietly. "It still feels strange having the title."

"You'll have to get used to it." George Campbell gave Stephen a nod. "You are the earl now, sir."

As if he needed reminding.

"Yes, George, you have my authority to trace whatever you need to. If you need papers signed for access, let me know."

"Will do, sir. And whatever the payments were, they weren't automatic withdrawals. The last one was a few months before your father died."

"So he was making them manually."

"It appears that way, for the moment, anyway."

Stephen nodded. "Do what you have to do. For over twenty-five years, someone was getting a piece of my father's money. I want to know who, and why."

George gave a nod and said his farewells. After he was gone, Stephen went back to his desk and sat heavily.

One thing he knew for sure. With his mother's recent health scare, he wasn't about to bring this to her attention unless he needed to. And certainly not until he got to the bottom of the…anomaly, as George put it. There was no need to alarm the family. It could be something entirely benign. His gut was telling him otherwise, but he wasn't so sure he trusted his gut these days.

He sighed and leaned back in the leather chair, closing his eyes. He'd never expected the earldom to weigh this heavily upon him.

Had his father felt the same when he'd inherited?

CHAPTER ONE

April

"ANEMONE, DO YOU have the data I was looking for this morning?"

Anemone looked up over her glasses and stared at her boss, Phillipe Leroux. She'd been seconded to his department a month ago, working as a liaison between Public Relations and his office in preparation for the launch of Aurora Inc.'s new fragrance. The launch was her baby, the first real project entrusted to her at the company, and she wasn't leaving any detail to chance.

Working at Aurora Inc. was a dream come true. The multinational company was a top name in fashion, cosmetics and jewelry. It was also run by the Pemberton family, including the new Earl of Chatsworth, Stephen Pemberton. Who also happened to be Anemone's half-brother.

Except Stephen didn't know that. None of the family knew that she was Cedric Pemberton's illegitimate daughter, and for the time being, she planned to keep it that way.

She reached for the file folder and handed it over. "All printed out for you, including pie charts and graphs with the latest results. Marketing sent it up straight away. The focus groups went well. I think you'll be pleased."

The launch of Aurora's new fragrance, Nectar, was scheduled for just over a week from now, and she knew that it was a particularly important moment for Phillipe, who was himself new to his position. His official title was Executive Manager of Fragrance, one step down from Director of Cosmetics and Fashion, who happened to be Will Pemberton. But Phillipe's education was in chemistry and his background in perfume. He'd been honest and said as much to her during their initial meeting and had expressed how he needed a strong assistant on his team. *No pressure, then*, she'd thought at the time, but she'd also been pleased that he thought she was that person—and that her former boss had recommended her for the temporary position.

Phillipe flipped through the file, giving the pages a quick glance. He looked up, his gray-blue eyes meeting hers. Her tummy always seemed to take a jolt when he did that. For the next two weeks, she reported to him directly, but that didn't stop her from noticing he was insanely attractive, with thick dark hair swept away from his face and a subtle smile that hinted at mischief. He was definitely more the intellectual type, but she'd always had a thing for brainy men. He looked down again and flipped through a few more pages, and she stared at his hands. Nice, big hands with long, graceful fingers.

She should not be having thoughts like this about her boss, no matter how temporary. Not if she wanted to keep this job and move up within the company. And she did want to keep it, she realized. She was relatively sure that if she showed up on the Pemberton doorstep and announced she was Cedric's daughter, she'd be thrown out on her ear. And that was the problem. She wanted to know her family, but she also genuinely loved working at Aurora. She was fairly certain she couldn't have both. So her secret would remain...her secret.

"Thank you, Anemone."

"Please call me Annie," she said, pushing her thoughts aside and smiling brightly at him. "Everyone calls me Annie." Over the years, she'd gotten used to having to spell her name immediately after giving it. She'd been working with Phillipe long enough now they could be on slightly more familiar terms, couldn't they?

"Annie," he said, and offered one of his small smiles. "This is great." He gestured with the file folder. "How am I set for the rest of the day?"

She brought up his schedule. "A meeting with William in an hour, then your afternoon is free from outside commitments." She looked up at him again. "I'm meeting with PR and Marketing later to iron out a few details, and then tweaking the catering menu for the launch."

"Fantastic." He leaned forward, resting his elbows on the counter in front of her desk. "I really appreciate how you've taken this event in hand."

She was determined not to blush at the praise.

He stepped back. "So, are you up for a field trip later today?"

She looked up, perplexed. "A field trip, Monsieur Leroux?"

He put the file down on the counter in front of her desk. "If I must call you Annie, then you must call me Phillipe." He leaned forward a little. "To be honest, I'm not sure I'll ever get used to this 'Monsieur Leroux' thing." He held her gaze. "I'm almost as new at my job as you are to yours. I like first names. And I think you and I are past being so formal, don't you?"

"All right...Phillipe."

Oh, my. It sounded so personal coming from her lips, perhaps because even after weeks on the job, she was still a little struck by him. He might be the brainy type, but he wore his suits incredibly well and she had yet to see him with a tie; he always left his shirt collar open at the throat. There was an understated sexiness beneath the surface that was incredibly attractive. "Where are we going?"

He grinned then, a much brighter smile than she was used to seeing. It was absolutely dazzling.

"I thought I'd take you to where we store our product and give you a crash course, seeing as the new fragrance is so close to launch."

Annie gave a quick nod. "That would be fine. Shall I book us a taxi for a specific time?"

"Let's leave it until I'm sure I can get away."

"Whatever you like. Just let me know when you're ready." She mentally raced through her tasks and wondered how many she could get through before lunch. She'd probably end up working through her break, but she didn't mind. Not really.

With a parting smile, Phillipe headed back toward his office.

Annie let out a long breath and put her forehead in her hands. This was not good. The best job she'd ever had included proximity to her secret family, and now she had to go and develop a crush on her boss. It wouldn't do at all. This had never been an issue before, and she'd been working in the clerical field for the past six years. But then, she'd never had a boss like Phillipe.

She wished she could go home, call her mum, and have a good chat about it, but that wasn't possible. Not anymore. Losing her mum had broken her heart. And even if it hadn't, finding out the truth about her father's identity would have. Two years too late to even meet him…

Which was why she had this job. Learning she was Cedric Pemberton's daughter had been a shock, and she knew his wife and children wouldn't take the news well. She wasn't even sure she was ever going to tell them. They were all the family she had in the world, but she didn't want to be *that person* who came in and dropped a massive bombshell. She knew how much that hurt. Her longing for family constantly warred with compassion for her father's wife and children—she certainly bore them no resentment. Perhaps she had to deal with never having known her father, but they were dealing with losing him. The situation wasn't their fault, after all. That was squarely on two people who couldn't be held accountable anymore: her mother, and Cedric Pemberton. Besides, telling the family wouldn't change anything, so what was the point?

If only Mum had told her earlier, she might have had an ally in all this. Instead, she'd found out in her mother's will.

Anemone was twenty-nine years old and an orphan. Her best friend, Rachael, lived in Norwich and Anemone had no partner to share this with. But if her mum could raise her alone, Anemone could do this. No decisions had been made about if and when she'd reveal her true identity. In the meantime, she was enjoying her job immensely and was discovering that the Pembertons were not the spoiled, entitled rich she'd expected. She liked them.

The phone rang, disturbing her thoughts, and she rolled her shoulders. She was being paid to do a job, not sit here angsting over a past that couldn't be changed. She touched her headset to answer the call and put the thoughts of the past behind her.

Phillipe ran a finger around his collar and scowled. This was damned inconvenient, wasn't it? He'd needed someone to take over the launch and Annie had come highly recommended from her boss in PR. Her steady temperament seemed to fit his own vibe and they worked well together. But in the weeks they'd been working together, he'd started to notice a lot more.

Like the way her hair curled over her shoulder when she left it down, the light brown flickering with auburn tints in the light. Or how blue her eyes were, even when she wore her cute glasses when she was working. She was amazingly efficient and often anticipated what he needed, which was utterly brilliant. And she was also surprisingly sweet, like when she'd said to call her Annie. Though he somehow preferred the name Anemone. It suited her—bright and cheerful and yet dainty and sweet.

He rolled his eyes. *Mon Dieu*, what was wrong with him? What a sappy thing to think.

He had much more important things to do, like make sure everything was set for the launch next week. This was his first one as a member of the senior management team, and he didn't want to let William down...or Bella, either. The Pemberton family had put a lot of trust in him when they'd promoted him to the executive team. He'd actually designed this particular scent two years ago. It was an odd bit of symmetry that had him in charge of its launch now.

Funny how much life could change in two short years.

He pushed those memories aside and focused on his day's itinerary instead. Today's trip to

Montparnasse would expose Annie to the wide variety of scents Aurora had to offer. If the lab were closer, he'd love to show her how scents were blended, but Grasse was too far a trip for a day. Instead, he'd show her the end product and try to explain the steps. If she were going to work in fragrance, she should understand it. While they were there, he'd look at the quality control reports and ensure everything was ready to ship next week. Nectar would initially only be available online or in Aurora stores. In six months, they'd expand distribution to an exclusive number of retailers worldwide.

So many details. There were times he seriously missed the lab. But getting out of Grasse had been a priority after his divorce, and when the opportunity had presented itself, he'd jumped at it.

A knock on the door pulled him out of his thoughts. "You ready for our meeting, Phillipe?"

He spun to find William leaning against the doorframe. "*Oui, bien sûr.* Sorry. Got lost in my thoughts for a moment there."

William chuckled. "I hope they were good thoughts. How are you finding things? I know we threw you into the deep end in the job."

"Slightly overwhelming," he admitted, putting his hands in his pockets. "But I'm managing. It's a learning curve, that's all." More than a learning curve. Throwing him into the "deep end," as William put it, had been a blessing, because his divorce had nearly drowned him and with the new position, he'd had to start swimming. The less time he had to think about Madelyn, the better. It was also why he shouldn't notice so much about Anemone. She worked for him, and he was still a wreck from the breakdown of his marriage. Two very good reasons to keep his distance.

"We're here to help," William said, sitting down across from Phillipe's desk. He opened up a folio. "Did you get the marketing reports this morning? They just sent copies to my office."

"Yes, Annie had them all printed out for me. The focus groups did very well. It's encouraging."

"It certainly is. The demographic data is quite illuminating…"

The meeting got underway, but Phillipe couldn't seem to erase the image of Anemone's blue eyes, looking at him through her spectacles.

He was in so much trouble.

Annie had never been to the storage facility in Montparnasse before. The building itself was rather nondescript, with a heavy double door that could be used as a loading dock. It certainly didn't have the polished glamour of the

Aurora shops or offices, but as Phillipe entered his security code for the front entrance, Annie felt a frisson of excitement. She was still awe-struck by the magnitude of the business, and it seemed she learned something more every day. This building was just one in the massive Aurora empire. And clearly, it was a favorite of Phillipe's. There was no hiding the excitement on his face.

"After you," he said, as the panel beeped, and the door unlocked.

There was a reception area just inside, and he signed them both in and accepted key cards. "*Merci*," he said to the receptionist, and then handed the ID over to Annie. "We keep tight security here. There's a lot of inventory."

"Are the perfumes made here?"

"No," he answered. "We have a facility in Grasse that manufactures and bottles the per-fume. We use this as a shipping base. Would you like to test some?"

She nodded, trying to keep her head from swiveling to and fro as they made their way fur-ther inside. There were no windows into any of the rooms, only steel doors that required a swipe of a card to enter. No marble counters or floors, just unforgiving concrete as their shoes clicked down a long hall. "Is there only perfume here?" she asked, hurrying to keep up.

"We keep our cosmetics here as well, the skin lines and the makeup. I'm still learning a lot of that part of the division. Scent is my wheelhouse." With his slight accent, the *h* was subtly dropped, and Annie was charmed.

He swiped his card and led her into another room. It was plain, but better than the gray, industrial-looking halls. The walls were white and held glass shelves. But the plainness was erased by the vast array of colorful bottles lining the shelves. Glass every shade of the rainbow glittered around them, and she stopped in her tracks.

"Oh. Oh, my."

He sent her one of those big smiles again. "It's beautiful, isn't it?"

Recessed lighting cast a golden hue over the bottles. "Stunning. These are all of Aurora's perfumes?"

"Indeed." He went to a nearby shelf and plucked off a dark blue bottle. "Indigo," he said, "released three years ago. For men *and* women. I used bergamot, cardamom, and sandalwood."

"You made this?"

"Yes. And several others here. Before I came to Paris, I led the team in Grasse."

"Which is the perfume capital of the world."

"Indeed." He smiled at her again. "You haven't been?"

"No, never," she replied, feeling rather provincial.

"We'll have to rectify that someday soon," he said. He put the bottle back on the shelf and gave her a tour of the room, explaining about the three "notes" to a scent—top, heart and base, and how the concentration of oil to alcohol and water made a scent a perfume, eau de toilette, or cologne.

There was a long counter on one side of the room and he led her there, then opened the cupboards beneath. "The bottles on the shelves are empty," he explained. "Light, heat… It can all change the life span of a scent. Humidity, too. Did you know that the worst place to store your perfume products is in your bathroom? Yet that is precisely where most people keep them." He shook his head as he pulled out a few bottles from the cupboard. "These are kept inside, where it is dark and cool. Let me choose a few for you to try."

He let her smell a few samples, setting them on the counter and spraying a strip of paper with the perfume and letting it dry before holding it close to her nose. "Not too many," he advised, "and you need to give your nose a break in between, or you'll get nose fatigue."

The term made her laugh, but she took in all he told her about the design of the bottles by superior glassmakers. Finally, he took out a stunning amber bottle with bubbles in the glass that made it appear effervescent. "That's the new one," she said, admiring the rich design. "The glass is even more beautiful in person."

"Exactly. It was created by a glassmaker in Biot, famous for their bubbled glass." He removed the top and sprayed another strip. "Tell me what you smell."

She took a slow sniff and let the scent envelop her. She closed her eyes. "Citrus, I think. And maybe… It's warm and sweet, like honey, with some sort of flower."

"You have a great nose," he pronounced. "The base notes aren't revealing themselves to you yet. But yes, blood orange at the top, and honey and jasmine in the heart notes. The base is patchouli and beeswax."

"Which is why it's called Nectar," she reasoned.

"Exactly. Though naming it certainly isn't my department. Hold out your wrist."

She did, and he misted it with the fragrance. "Your top notes will be immediately apparent. But as the day goes on, you'll be able to see how the scent changes with your own body chemistry."

She lifted her wrist and inhaled the warm, soft scent. "This is lovely, Phillipe."

"It is one of my favorites."

"You designed this, too?"

"I did, two years ago. I'm delighted it's finally going to market." He sighed. "It was the last one I mixed. After that, I moved up to running the entire facility and was more hands-off." His eyes took on a faraway quality, and to her surprise, she thought she detected a flash of pain on his face.

"You miss it."

He smiled at her. "Very much. Don't get me wrong, I like the new job and it's a fabulous opportunity. But my heart will always be in the lab with the oils."

He clapped his hands together then, dispelling the mood. "Come. There's more for you to see."

By the time they finished the tour, it was after five and Annie's stomach was growling. She'd only packed some fruit for her lunch, as her fridge was nearly bare and she was trying to economize, and she'd eaten at her desk, trying to plow through her tasks. She'd never thought she'd live the starving-student diet at this point in her life, but the rent on her studio flat ate up most of her earnings. Thankfully, the seconded position came with a premium added to her regular salary. There was only so much ramen a girl could eat.

"Well, this is where we part, I guess," Phillipe said, as they stepped outside into the spring air. "Shall I get you a taxi to take you home?"

They weren't going back to the office, then. And Annie's budget wouldn't strain to cover a cab, not if she wanted to eat at all in the next few days. Walking was out of the question; she was in her heels, and it was a good three miles back to her flat. "Oh, no need," she said, making her voice breezy. "I'll catch the train."

He frowned. "But it is rush hour. How far away are you?"

Nerves bubbled in her belly. She'd managed to keep her situation private during her few months in Paris. Once she'd got the job—a miraculous feat in itself—she'd had to sort out logistics. "Only in the third arrondissement," she said lightly. "I really only have to change once. I'll be fine, truly."

"But surely a taxi is much quicker and easier." He lifted his hand to hail one, and Annie reached to pull down his arm.

"Truly, I'm just as happy taking transit."

He stared at her for a long moment as a cab drove by, not slowing. She saw the second he understood because his eyes softened. "We don't pay you enough," he said softly. "I'm sorry, Annie. I never thought."

"It's fine. I'm no different than a million other working women in the city. I have a budget and a cozy place to live, and I can afford transit easier than cab fare. It's real life, that's all." She thought of her mum, struggling to put food on the table with her meager salary. If Annie had understood, she would have insisted on fewer treats and nice things. It was no surprise that there'd been nothing left at the end.

There was no point in thinking about it now. As she was fond of saying, "It is what it is." She just had to work with what she had.

"It was inconsiderate of me. Especially because I seem to be taking my newfound status for granted. Please, take a cab, and expense it. You were here for work."

But it hadn't felt like work. It had felt like a lovely afternoon exploring something new with an incredibly alluring companion. She tucked a loose strand of hair behind her ear. "All right." She relented, because she could tell he honestly felt bad about it. And he was right about one thing—it was rush hour, and the trains would be packed. She'd be home in less than half an hour this way.

Since the initial cab had passed, they'd not seen another, so they walked toward the metro station, where they would be sure to find a cabstand. The air was mild with the promise of spring, and sunny. Annie was finding spring in Paris to be every bit as lovely as she'd heard, and it wasn't a hardship walking next to Phillipe, either.

"When did you first move to Paris?" he asked, making conversation.

She tucked her hair again; the light breeze kept ruffling it in front of her face. "Last October when I took the job in the PR department. I was in Guildford before that…outside of London. I lived with my mum and commuted into the city for work."

"Your mother must miss you," he mused.

She swallowed against a lump in her throat. "My mum died nearly a year ago. She had a brain aneurysm. Nothing we could do, no warning."

He stopped, then took her hand in his. "Oh, Anemone. I'm so sorry. What a horrible thing. Do you have any other family?"

"I never had any brothers or sisters, and my grandparents passed on when I was a teenager." She smiled up at him. "It's okay, truly. I wanted a fresh start and here I am. My story tends to be a bit of a downer. How about you? Are you liking being in Paris?"

He accepted her change of subject and shrugged. "It's not quite home for me yet. I grew up in Grasse, and I miss it."

"You left people behind?"

His jaw tightened. Not a lot, but just enough

that she noticed, and she wished she could take back the question. "My parents. But no one else who would miss me."

Her curiosity spiked. There was a lot in what he wasn't saying, and she figured a relationship had gone wrong. By her best guess, Phillipe had to be in his midthirties. She'd noticed right off that he didn't wear a wedding ring. But that didn't mean much in the overall scheme of things. One didn't have to have a ring to have their heart trampled on.

"I'm sure that's not true." She couldn't imagine someone not loving Phillipe. He was kind, smart, handsome…the total package, really, when all was said and done. And he was successful. He had a lot to offer someone. "And anyway, her loss."

He turned his head sharply to look at her. "Who said there was a woman?"

"Your face did." She lifted an eyebrow. "Unless I'm completely wrong."

He sighed. "You're not wrong. My divorce was finalized, oh, a year and a half ago now. I'm afraid I haven't quite left all my bitterness behind."

She thought for a moment as they made their way along the sidewalk that was growing more crowded the closer they got to the station. "I think we all have wounds that take longer to heal than we'd like," she finally said. "Don't be too tough on yourself."

They reached the cabstand and stood in the short line. "I find that hard to believe of you." He shoved his hands in his pockets again and met her gaze. "You don't strike me as the bitter type. Or someone who indulges in self-pity."

"You'd be surprised."

"What are you bitter about, Anemone Jones?"

She looked up at him and took a breath. There was a lot, and while she tried to keep positive, some days resentments did sneak in. She was human, after all. "I never knew my father," she admitted. "Never even knew who he was until my mother died. And then I found out he'd died before her, so now I'll never know him at all."

Phillipe's gaze softened. "I'm sorry," he said quietly. "That's rough."

"I try not to let it get me down, but there are times when I can't help but think what if." She shrugged. "So I get it. Moving on is hard."

The couple ahead of them got in their cab and Phillipe and Annie stepped ahead, waiting for the next car. It took no time at all for one to arrive, and they slid into the back seat. "Let's drop you at yours, and then I can go on to my place and pay for the entire trip with the company card."

"Thank you," she said quietly, but then realized her boss was going to notice that she lived in a very plain walk-up apartment. Then again, what did it matter? He already knew she was finding it very tight financially. She had to let her pride go sometime.

She gave her address, and the car began zipping its way through traffic. "So," Phillipe said, "on a lighter topic, the launch party next week. You are coming, yes?"

Her eyes widened. The launch of Nectar was a posh event in a ballroom with catered food and champagne and beautiful people. She should know; she was organizing it. She certainly didn't belong there.

"Oh, I don't think so. I'm pretty sure assistants don't usually attend these things."

"But I think you should. You're part of the team and you dived right in with the planning and details. This wouldn't be happening at all if not for you."

She looked him dead in the eye. "Do I look like I would fit in there?"

He stared back. "Do I?"

She imagined him in a tuxedo and bit down on her lip. "Actually, yes."

"Well, I don't feel it. I'll make a confession— half the time I feel like an imposter, and one day William and Bella and the other Pembertons are going to figure out that I'm not management material."

She shook her head. "Nonsense. They wouldn't have trusted you with the position if they didn't think you could do it. Besides, you probably already have a tuxedo and shiny shoes."

He laughed and rested his head against the back of the seat. "Well, yes, I do." He turned his head. "So come with me. We can go as a work team. It's much better than trying to find a plus-one. If we get bored, we can have an impromptu staff meeting." He grinned and she couldn't help but smile back. "Consider it moral support."

"I'll think about it," she replied, because what woman in her right mind could say no to Phillipe Leroux?

"Excellent."

A little curl of excitement took up residence in her belly. She imagined the ballroom, and the glittering lights and crystal glasses of champagne, hors d'oeuvres that she'd ordered but couldn't pronounce, and beautiful dresses and shoes. But just like that, her excitement dissipated, and she came to earth with a thud.

How could she attend an Aurora Inc. function in nothing but a little black dress she'd bought on the high street? And there were no funds to buy something new and appropriate—it would cost her an entire month's rent.

The truth settled in, harsh and deep. She might have a place at Aurora Inc., but she would never be a Pemberton. She might as well face up to that now.

CHAPTER TWO

IT WAS JUST as well that Annie didn't let her fantasies run away with her, because the next day she was called to the fifth floor and the executive offices for a meeting. When she'd asked if it was for her to attend with Phillipe, Stephen Pemberton's assistant said that, no, only she was required and to please go to the small boardroom.

She couldn't imagine what it could be about, so she grabbed her phone and shoved her laptop into her bag in case she needed to take notes or bring up any files. Then she made her way up to the executive offices.

She wasn't a stranger to the floor; she dealt with William's and Bella's assistants often enough. But to meet with Stephen—he was COO and head of acquisitions. It all felt very strange, and she knocked on the boardroom door before opening it a little.

"Miss Jones. Come in."

Stephen Pemberton was intimidating at the best of times, with his tall frame, strong jaw and dark features. He wasn't smiling as she opened the door and stepped inside, and then discovered the whole of the Pemberton family seated at the table, looking at her strangely.

Her gaze settled on Aurora, the matriarch of the family. Her normally placid features looked shaken, her face pale, and her eyes uncertain.

They know.

Somehow they knew. She could feel it in the slow, sickening twist of her stomach, the way they stared at her with barely veiled hostility. How had they found out? She'd said nothing. As far as she was aware, not a soul knew she was Cedric's daughter. But to appear before the entire Pemberton family? There was only one possible reason.

She wanted to turn and run, but where would she run to? Nowhere. So she swallowed against the fear in her throat and stood in the doorway, unmoving, feeling rather like a trapped animal.

"Miss Jones," Stephen began, his voice steady. "Anemone Jones, daughter of Catherine Jones?"

"Ye—" She tried to speak, and the word caught. She cleared her throat and tried again, determined to be strong. "Yes." Better.

"You were born in Guildford?"

She nodded. "Yes." She made herself look directly at him because she couldn't bear to see the expressions on everyone else's faces. She'd walked right into an ambush, hadn't she?

"And you're twenty-nine."

"Just turned."

"It's not true." Charlotte stood, and Annie looked over at her. Hatred flew like sparks from Charlotte's eyes. "You're six months younger than I am, and you are not Cedric Pemberton's daughter!"

"Sit down, Charlotte," Stephen said sharply.

To Annie's surprise, Charlotte sat, but the hostility in the room rose substantially.

"Please shut the door, Miss Jones," Stephen said, though despite the word *please*, it wasn't exactly polite.

She had to explain, but she didn't know where to start. Panic threaded like ice through her veins. How this had happened was a thought for another time. Right now, she had to keep her focus on answering questions as best she could. She had done absolutely nothing wrong. The thought grounded her. As she was trying to find the words to respond, Aurora spoke from the end of the table with quiet authority.

"How much do you want?"

Annie's gaze shifted to look at the older

woman. "Oh, no, it's not like that. I don't want anything."

Aurora scoffed. "Please, Miss Jones. It's always like that."

How sad that the Pemberton automatic default was that everyone must want something from them.

"Do you plan to contest the will?" This from Bella, who seemed the least antagonistic of anyone in the room, her posture attentive but not on edge, her words measured.

"What? No," Annie said, looking at her, hoping to find a partial ally in this ambush. "Of course not. Not at all. I didn't even know myself until after Cedric had passed. I never knew who my father was growing up. Mum refused to say." It had been the thing she'd resented most. Her mum had said it was to protect her and to protect her father, but it had always felt as if a piece was missing. And to find out after his death had been cruelly harsh. Her gaze darted from face to face. "How did you find out? I never intended—"

"Never intended what?" Charlotte demanded. "This was calculated. You're working here. You have access to any number of things. Just what were you planning?"

"Yes, why are you here, at Aurora?" William took a turn to speak. "You've been working here since October. To what end? Make money selling our secrets to the tabloids, perhaps?"

She swallowed against the tightening in her throat, suddenly angry at the unjust accusations. What kind of world did they live in where everyone was suspected of horrible motives? "I wanted…" She took a moment for a breath, to consider her words. "I just wanted to know more about you. I did not intend to create any problems with the family. Exactly the opposite, actually." She took a breath and looked at Bella. "You're all assigning motives that don't exist. I only wanted to get to know who you were. I never wanted to turn anyone's world upside down."

She took a moment, considered that perhaps the truth would work best, even if it made her vulnerable. "I just… I don't have anyone. My mum died last year."

"Yes, we know."

The blunt, emotionless reply was from Stephen, and she swiveled around. "You know?"

"Of course we do. When I discovered who you really were, I did some digging. And whatever you say about not wanting anything, you're lying. The money stopped flowing when our father died. You must miss that biannual deposit." He dropped his gaze to her simple skirt and blouse, assessing. "Whatever did you do with the money, anyway?"

Annie stared as her lips fell open. "What money?"

"Come, come, Miss Jones. Let's not play dumb." Aurora's smooth voice cut through the heavy silence.

Annie's mind spun. She'd never seen any money. She supposed it had all gone to her mum, really. And what had Mum done with it? There certainly wasn't any left now. Oh, goodness…the little trips, the treats and tickets to concerts, little shopping days… Had that all been Cedric's money?

"I don't understand," she said. "When Mum died, I was her sole beneficiary. Believe me, there was nothing left, not by the time I paid the funeral costs. We rented a little house in Guildford, certainly nothing extravagant."

But there'd miraculously been money for her to go to school in London for a year. And they had never been hungry or cold—their lifestyle had been modest but not poor. She'd gone to a decent school. She'd taken piano lessons. She'd always thought her mum had been a whiz at budgeting on her small salary, but now she wondered if Cedric had indeed been topping up the coffers.

She looked at Aurora. "I swear to you, Mrs.

Pemberton, I never knew anything about your husband until Mum died. I just wanted…" She cleared her throat of any emotion and tried again. "I applied for a job here because I wanted to know a little more about him. Not for any nefarious reasons. Not to extort you."

No, she thought to herself. *To feel as if I'm not so very alone in the world.*

She pushed back the thought before it could unravel her any further. "I thought if I could meet his family, I might be able to…"

She stopped. The next words sitting on the tip of her tongue would make her sound utterly foolish. "I'm sorry," she finished.

Stephen took a step closer. "You thought you might be able to what, Miss Jones?"

"It doesn't matter." It was over now, wasn't it? She'd had her glimpse of her father's family and had a great job for six whole months. She didn't want to start over again, but she didn't have much of a choice.

"I think it matters very much," said Bella. "What did you want to be able to do?"

Being held to account by the very intimidating Pemberton clan was tough; deliberately making herself even more vulnerable was excruciating. Her heart pounded painfully as she stood silently before them, being judged.

Maybe her methods had been flawed, but her

motives were pure. Not that they'd believe her, but she knew it in her heart. "I thought I might get to know him a little by knowing you. And I knew if I came to you claiming to be his daughter, I would never get the chance. Was that a mistake? Possibly. But what would have happened if I'd come out of the woodwork, making this claim? What would you have done?"

Stephen raised an eyebrow. "Exactly what I did when the discrepancy showed up in the accounts. Investigated. And shown you the door."

"Stephen," Bella said quietly.

"Yes, exactly," Annie agreed. She turned to Aurora. The woman was powerful and intimidating with all her calm strength, but Annie detected a crack in the facade, a flash of uncertainty in the set of her lips. "I'm sorry, Mrs. Pemberton. I know this must be hurting you terribly. Part of the reason I kept this secret was because I truly did not want to hurt anyone, you most of all. He was your husband and—"

"I knew," she interrupted, her voice like steel covered in velvet.

A hush fell over the room.

"Maman," Stephen said, staring at her. Every eye in the room focused on the woman who maintained such a stoic posture.

"What, Stephen?" Aurora turned cold, gray eyes on her son. "I did not know the details. But

I knew about the affair. I knew there'd been a child. And I knew he'd sent money. If you had come to me with your concerns, I could have helped you. But you kept me in the dark."

"But today..." He ran his hand through his hair. "When I told you about this, and asked to set up the meeting..."

Her lips thinned. "I wanted to see for myself. I wanted to see Anemone and I wanted to hear her answers. And now I have."

Charlotte stood again. "I want a paternity test."

"Agreed," said William.

Aurora sighed. Annie desperately wanted to sit down; the adrenaline was still coursing through her system and she was feeling quite wobbly, but she knew she couldn't sit so she took even breaths as she stood before what felt like her jury.

"I agree to take a test," she said clearly, lifting her chin.

"Good," said Aurora, nodding at her with what could be considered a touch of approval. "Though you have his eyes. And you're wearing his mother's locket."

Her hand went to her neck where the silver pendant lay warm against her skin.

"Give it back."

Annie turned startled eyes toward Charlotte,

whose hostility was plain in the angry flash of her eyes and flush of her skin. "That was my grandmother's. Give it back."

"Charlotte," Aurora snapped.

Tears finally stung Annie's eyes. The locket was all she had of her father. But he was also a father she had never known. Charlotte, William, Bella and Stephen had grown up with him. They had memories to cherish. What claim did she have, other than blood? Her lip quivered and she reached for the clasp at her neck. She didn't deserve a family heirloom.

She held it for one last moment in her palm, then put it down on the boardroom table.

"It would be best for you to clean out your desk today," Stephen suggested, firmly, but not harshly. "And I would advise you not to go to the press."

As if she would. If she'd wanted to, she could have sold her story ages ago and had plenty of money. Everyone in the room knew that she could have asked for anything and had asked for nothing.

So she lifted her chin a little more. "You know, your actions today are exactly why I never told you in the first place. I knew this would happen. And perhaps you're not wrong. It's a horrible thing, a family secret like this." She thought of Phillipe and his animated face just yesterday, showing her the different fragrances in Montparnasse. The launch of Nectar meant so much to him. Right now she wasn't feeling any particular loyalty toward the Pembertons, but she didn't want to let him down. She made a snap decision and chose to focus on Bella as she spoke.

"But I should remind you that you have a major launch next week, and I'm the only one who knows all the details. It would be unfair to the other staff for me to abandon them now, and utterly unfair to Phillipe, who has so much at stake. I'll make you a deal. I'll take your paternity test and I keep my job until the launch. After that I'll pack up my desk and be gone."

There was silence in the room, then Stephen spoke up. "I don't think you're in any position to call the shots here, Miss Jones."

She kept her gaze on Bella. "Am I not?"

Everyone present knew that she was carrying a PR grenade and all she had to do to pull the pin was go to the press.

"I agree to your terms." Bella gave a short nod.

"Bella!" That outburst was from Charlotte, who seemed particularly distressed about Annie's existence. But who could blame her? Aurora had been pregnant with her while Cedric had been having an affair with Annie's mother. She was entitled to her feelings. Annie reminded herself again that none of this had been her fault.

"Next Friday, then," Stephen said, his voice slightly hoarse. "Next Friday you'll be gone."

"Agreed. Now if there's nothing else, I need to get back to work."

Annie was greeted with silence, so she turned on her heel and left the boardroom.

All the way down the hall she kept her composure. Down a floor and back to her desk, she never wavered. But when Phillipe came around the corner and took one look at her face, he stopped short.

"Annie?" he said, his eyes wide with concern.

And then her tightly maintained composure crumpled, the first sob came out, and she found herself wrapped in his arms.

Phillipe had no idea what had just happened. One moment he was coming out to ask Annie a question, and the next he was holding her as she cried against his shoulder. What on earth could have happened?

"Come into my office where it's more private," he murmured in her ear, stepping back a bit but keeping a steadying hand beneath her elbow. "Come, Annie. It's all right."

She gave a shaky nod and followed him. Once inside his office, he shut the door and guided her toward a chair. "What can I get you? Water? Tea?"

"Nothing, thank you. I'm so sorry. I can't believe I started to cry." The reply was punctuated with sniffs, so he retrieved a box of tissues from the little bathroom off his office and handed it to her.

She took three and dabbed her eyes, then blew her nose.

Phillipe pulled up another chair so he was sitting near her, rather than behind his desk. "When you're ready, tell me what happened."

It took a few moments, and another blow of her nose, before she seemed to trust herself enough to speak.

"It's such a long story," she said softly. "I'll be fine. But you should know... I'm leaving Aurora after the launch."

"What?" Phillipe ran a hand over his face. "Why?" She was sitting in his office, her face red from crying, looking absolutely defeated. What on earth could have happened? This morning everything was fine.

"I expected it would happen if..." She paused.

"If what?"

When she stayed firmly silent, he moved his chair a little closer. "Annie, please tell me what's happened. You can trust me."

"I know I can." She lifted her chin and met

his gaze. She looked utterly miserable. "But you're going to look at me differently, and I'm not going to like that."

"Let me be the judge of that," he said, but a flicker of unease went through him. Keeping secrets was high on his list of disliked behaviors. Right up there with betrayal and lying. They all seemed to go together, somehow.

"Don't say I didn't warn you." She twisted her fingers in her lap, then met his gaze. "They— the Pembertons—found out who my father is."

He drew his brows together. "So what? What does your father have to do with anything?"

"My father," she said slowly, "was Cedric Pemberton."

Phillipe sat back in his chair. Of anything Annie could have told him this morning, this wouldn't even have made the top one hundred. Her, Cedric Pemberton's daughter? "I don't understand."

"My mother had an affair with him. I am the product of that affair."

"And you work here, but they never knew about you?"

She shook her head. "Apparently Aurora knew I existed but didn't know it was me. And I wasn't going to say anything, either. I just wanted to know who they are. I don't have any other family, you see. But I knew if I told them, I'd never get a chance to know them at all."

"So you lied to them."

"Yes," she whispered. "Because I didn't want to hurt anyone."

Phillipe got up from his chair and paced to the other side of the room. *I lied because I didn't want to hurt you.* Those words had been Madelyn's and he still hated them. As if she'd somehow spared his delicate feelings. He balled his fingers into tense fists, then let them go again.

"How did they find out?" He should just let her go. He loathed the idea of someone pretending to be who they weren't. She'd got the job under false pretenscs, then. Now she was key staff to a major launch. What an unholy mess. "Did they fire you?"

She blew her nose once more and her face took on a stubborn set. "No. I agreed to leave after the launch. As far as how they found out, apparently my father paid my mother money for years, though I didn't know about that. Stephen tracked the money and discovered me."

"I see."

She stood and folded her hands in front of her. "Do you? Really? Because if it was money I wanted I could have gone to them and contested the will. I could have asked them for money to go away. I could have sold my story to the papers. I didn't do any of those things, Phillipe. I just wanted to get to know them. I discovered a job I really loved and one that I'm good at. And as of next Friday, that's all over."

He thought for a moment. She was right about one thing. If she'd wanted money, she could have gone after it in a variety of ways. He'd seen where she lived. *Modest* was a generous descriptor of her building and one would assume the flats within. She took transit to save money. And while he was no expert in fashion—fragrance was his thing—he knew that despite her tidy and professional appearance, she didn't have a high-end wardrobe.

Money had not been her objective, then. Was she telling him the truth about wanting to know her family? Or was she playing on his sympathies?

"Charlotte insisted on a paternity test. I agreed to it." She wiped her hands over her face. "I'm so sorry I broke down in front of you. It was just delayed emotion from being ambushed. I had no idea what was coming until I stepped into the boardroom this morning and they were all there."

"You're really Cedric Pemberton's daughter."

"I am. Stephen wanted me out of here today, but I'm staying until after the event." She met his gaze and he saw steel under the sweetness. "When I take something on, I see it through. Now, speaking of, I have a lot of work to get through this afternoon. I should get back to it."

She was almost to his door when he called out. "Annie, wait."

She turned around, but her lips were set, and he noticed her hand shaking on the doorknob. She was putting on a good show of strength, but he could tell she was barely holding it together.

"They can't fire you. I don't think they'd risk the chance of a wrongful dismissal suit."

She shrugged. "Technically I did nothing wrong, but I wasn't honest, either. And I won't stay where I'm not wanted or valued."

She lifted her chin and then stepped out of his office.

He let her go.

CHAPTER THREE

PHILLIPE SAT AT his desk for nearly an hour, trying to sort through what Annie had told him. She was Cedric Pemberton's illegitimate daughter. She'd started a job here under false pretenses. She'd lied.

He tapped his pen on the file cover in front of him and frowned. She'd also said that she didn't want to hurt anyone. Was it true? What did it say about him that he wanted to believe her? Was he truly that gullible? Taken in by a pretty face and some tears? It wasn't like he hadn't done that before. Only Madelyn had had the power to stomp all over his heart. Anemone Jones did not.

It also wouldn't be fair for him to judge her based on his ex-wife's behavior. The truth was, she was a damned good employee, and she was going to be out of a job. Simply because of who her father was.

Who she claims he is, Phillipe reminded himself, but seeing her tears, remembering their conversations… He believed her. Granted, being secretive about it was probably not the best decision. That one point made him more uneasy than anything.

He tossed the pen on his desk, shrugged on his suit jacket, and made his way upstairs to William's office. William was one of the fairest men Phillipe had ever met. Phillipe wanted to get the Pemberton perspective before forming a definitive opinion.

William was seated at his desk, staring at a computer monitor, when Phillipe knocked on the doorframe. Will looked up and gave a grim smile. "I wondered when you'd be to see me. I'm actually surprised it took this long."

"I found myself comforting a distraught employee," Phillipe said, stepping inside. "I thought it would be good to get a full picture of what happened."

"It's a hell of a business, Phillipe. How much do you know?"

"Her side…or rather, her perspective. I'm not fond of choosing sides."

Will looked at him for a long moment, until Phillipe grew uncomfortable with the scrutiny. Talking about personal lives wasn't something they did. Will knew that Phillipe was divorced but nothing else. Certainly none of the sordid details, and he'd like to keep it that way.

"You know, then, that she claims to be my half-sister."

"Indeed." Phillipe gestured toward a chair and Will nodded in an unspoken invitation to take a seat.

"She can't work here, Phillipe. You know that. She got this job—"

"Under false pretenses. I know." Phillipe finished Will's sentence. "She didn't disclose who she was."

"Who she claims to be," Will corrected.

The family was taking a hard line on this, it seemed. Will was a fairly easygoing guy, but Phillipe got the sense that he wasn't going to budge an inch where Miss Jones was concerned.

"She said she agreed to a paternity test. She must be confident that the results will show she's Cedric's daughter."

"What else is she going to say?" Will asked.

Phillipe sat back in the chair and studied his boss. It was no secret that when something went awry with the family, Will tended to step up and do damage control. As far as Phillipe was aware, that was how he'd come to marry his wife, Gabi Baresi—by keeping her out of the eyes of the press after a major scandal.

"Has she asked for anything? Money to keep quiet, that sort of thing?"

Will shook his head. "No. Which makes me nervous. She said something about wanting to be close to us because she has no family." He angled a wry glance at Phillipe. "I'm sorry, but I'm distrustful of a sob story."

"Maybe it's true," Phillipe replied, surprising himself by coming to her defense. Still, he'd been the one holding her in his arms earlier. She would have to be a very good actress to fake that kind of emotion. He simply couldn't believe it of her.

"Perhaps you don't understand." Will's jaw tightened. "It's difficult to give anyone the benefit of the doubt in our position. There are always those who want something from us. Who are just looking for a juicy detail to sell to the press. Trust is a rare commodity."

"If she is Cedric's daughter—"

"Then we'll deal with that. As a family."

The message was clear: this was none of his business. The dismissal grated on him.

"You should let her keep her job."

"Stephen will never agree."

"With due respect, Will, it's not up to only Stephen."

Will sat back. "The family has to agree, however." He tapped his fingers on the desk, a little wrinkle forming between his brows as he thought. "You know, though, maybe it would be better to have her here. Certainly easier to keep an eye on her."

Phillipe knew coming upstairs had been a long shot. He decided to remain silent, rather than push his case, and let Will's brain take over.

After several long seconds, Will nodded. "Let me talk to Bella. Stephen's a hothead about this and Bella's the CEO." He tapped his fingers on the desk. "We should have the paternity results by the launch. But if the results are negative—"

"Then she lied, and I won't stand in your way." Phillipe knew there was no guarantee Bella would agree, and even if she did, there was no way of knowing if Annie would want to work here after today's debacle. "I'm just asking you to put yourself in her shoes, if she is Cedric's daughter, and treat her fairly."

"I'm always fair."

Phillipe knew that to be true, at least in his interactions with Will. And he didn't want to push his case too far. She'd negotiated a way to stay until the launch and he didn't want to jeopardize that. But there was part of him that could relate to Annie being the underdog here. He'd felt much the same way when he'd entered Madelyn's family sphere—a very different class from his upbringing. Always feeling *less*, and at a disadvantage. No matter how much he tried to make it otherwise.

"Thank you for hearing me out," he offered, standing and holding out his hand.

Will shook it. "You're doing a great job, Phillipe. I know it's been a steep learning curve, moving from mixing to running the lab and now corporate. Don't minimize all you've accomplished. No matter what happens, the launch will go forward, and your department will have the support it needs."

"Thanks," Phillipe answered, and shook Will's hand. But after he left and headed back to his own office, he wondered why he'd felt so compelled to fight for Annie. Was it just because she'd cried on his shoulder? Was he that vulnerable to a crying woman? He rather suspected it was something more. Like making sure she didn't go through this by herself, the way he'd had to. If nothing else, Annie would not be alone. Not if he could help it.

Annie sat in her flat and stared out the window. She couldn't seem to get up the gumption to do anything this afternoon. Normally, she'd be at work, at her desk and working her way through her sizable to-do list. Instead, she was sitting at home—such as it was—and unable to focus on anything. She could read a book or perhaps take a walk along the river, but instead she was staring at the street below wondering what her next steps should be. Nothing, she supposed, until the paternity results came back. Just thirty minutes ago she'd given a swab to a nurse, officially witnessed by a member of the Aurora legal team. What did they think? That she'd fake the sample?

The family's treatment of her hadn't exactly been a surprise, but it had been more acrimonious than she'd hoped. For months she'd worked at Aurora and the Pemberton family had only ever been pleasant and fair. This was a different circumstance, she acknowledged to herself. Especially for her half-siblings. It wasn't just her existence but what it meant that had to hurt them. That their father—the man they'd idolized—had fathered a child while Aurora had already been pregnant. What a devastating blow. She had always been sensitive to that. It wasn't that she didn't understand. She did. She just wasn't the one to blame and didn't like being treated as the enemy.

So what now? Did she leave Paris? To do so would also mean leaving the Pembertons behind. Aurora Inc. was headquartered here, even though they had the manor house back in England and Charlotte lived in Richmond most of the time. Annie had no place to go if she went home; she'd given up the lease on her mother's house and put their belongings in storage. She couldn't go back without a job.

Or should she find another position here, in Paris? It meant staying in this cramped flat, and she'd never land as great a position as she had at Aurora. And it wasn't as if the Pembertons would give her a glowing reference. Phillipe might, she realized, and her cheeks heated.

Yesterday she'd utterly humiliated herself by bursting into tears. She'd always been like that…holding her emotions in and simply dealing with stress until a breaking point where the dam of overwhelm broke and came out her eyes. To do so in front of Phillipe was mortifying, both because he was her boss and because he was…well… She bit down on her lip. Phillipe Leroux was an incredibly attractive, successful man. She'd have to be blind not to notice and respond. And his hug yesterday had been so reassuring, so gentle, and yet strong and sure.

She was going to miss the job. She was also going to miss working for Phillipe. Oh, it had only been a temporary assignment to his department, but still.

Annie went to the stove and put on the kettle, then cleaned out the coffee press and added fresh grounds. Learning how to make proper coffee had been life changing, and when the kettle whistled, she poured in the boiling water. In three minutes she'd push down the plunger and have it just the way she liked—hot and strong.

She had just gotten her mug out of the cupboard when the buzzer to her apartment rang. She hadn't placed any orders so it couldn't be a delivery. The DNA test had already been completed. Had they forgotten something?

"Bonjour," she said into the intercom.

"Bonjour, Annie. *C'est* Phillipe.*"*

Phillipe! What was he doing here? She bit on her lower lip in consternation. She was in ratty yoga pants and a T-shirt from the last concert she'd gone to with Rachael. "Come up," she said, not knowing what else to do.

She grabbed the elastic holding back her ratty ponytail and quickly pulled her hair back neatly, twisting it deftly and hoping it looked marginally better. There was no time to change.

Why was he here?

The knock came too quickly, and she let out a breath and smoothed her hands over her face. She opened the door and put on a smile, then hoped her tongue didn't roll out of her mouth.

He had on jeans, a shirt unbuttoned at the collar, and a blue sport coat. He looked delicious.

He glanced at her T-shirt and a slow grin crawled up his cheek. "Nice," he offered, meeting her eyes, his own warm with humor. "But not suitable for the office."

Heat rushed to her face. She stepped back and opened the door wider, inviting him in. "I just made coffee. Would you like some?"

"That would be lovely, thank you."

She left him standing there and went to the tiny kitchen to pour the coffee into two cups. Weeks of working with him had taught her he took his black, like hers, so in mere moments she was back, handing him a cup, and gesturing to the tiny sofa—the only piece of living room furniture that fit in the studio apartment.

"You're rather cozy here," he said, a smile turning up one corner of his mouth.

"*Cozy* is a nice word for it," she replied, and took a seat on the sofa. He sat next to her; the sofa was so small that only a few inches separated them. Everything felt…confined.

He chuckled. "I had a studio flat when I was studying. A bed, a couple of chairs, and that was it."

"I bet you don't now," she said, then could have bitten her tongue. She didn't mean to get snippy about his success.

His dark eyes held hers for a few moments. "No," he said quietly, "I don't. And you wouldn't, either, if you'd made any claim on Cedric's estate."

"You're not suggesting that I—"

"No, not at all!" He held up a hand. "I just mean that I believe what you told me yesterday. You don't have to live like this. If you'd wanted money, you could have leveraged this in many ways. But you didn't."

Relief rushed through her, taking away some of the heavy weight on her shoulders. "Thank you," she breathed, cradling her cup. "That means a lot, Phillipe."

"But you can understand the Pembertons' skepticism."

"Of course! I expected nothing less, to be honest. I mean, if I put myself in their shoes, I would have done exactly the same thing. Maybe more." She hesitated, then looked at him over her mug. "I hope this isn't rude, but why are you here?"

"I was worried. You booked this afternoon as a sick day, but you looked fine this morning. I was worried something had happened."

"Oh! No, not at all." She smiled at him. "Actually, the Pembertons don't waste any time. I came home and had my swab this afternoon. Now we wait."

"You're still leaving after the launch?"

She raised an eyebrow. "Yes. I'm lucky that they agreed to let me stay until the end of next week."

Phillipe took a sip of his coffee, then shifted on the sofa and met her gaze again. "Actually, about that. I spoke to Will yesterday. You're very good at your job. I suggested they should let you stay on. If—"

The cup shook in her hand. "If my test is positive."

"Yes." He gave a brisk nod. "But even if you leave next week, I'll make sure you have a glowing reference to help you get another job."

"I don't know what to say." Or feel, she realized. It was incredible to think that he'd gone to Will Pemberton to plead her case. She'd been right in her assessment from the beginning: Phillipe Leroux was a good man, and fair. More than fair. For someone who felt unsure in his own position, it said a lot that he'd been willing to vouch for her. "Why would you risk your own position for me? Not that I think they would fire you, I mean," she said, starting to stutter a little. "I just mean… Well, Will is your boss. You put yourself in an awkward position just talking to him on my behalf."

"Because it's what's fair," he said simply. "If you are Cedric's daughter, they can't just turn you out in the cold. And to be honest, I don't think they would. That's not the family I know. They just need time to come to grips with it."

Now Phillipe was looking at her with what

appeared to be hope, which also seemed unreal. She was nobody. Nobody! But somehow Phillipe Leroux had made her out to be someone important. Someone valuable. That was a very new feeling.

Aurora's words echoed in her head, and she sighed. "Aurora did say I have his eyes."

Phillipe was quiet for a bit and sipped his coffee. It was one of the things she'd noticed about him over the past weeks. He said what he needed to, but then often sat back and waited for others to speak, and then he listened.

Phillipe was a difficult man to resist. Smart, charming, but also kind. Slightly intimidating—he was educated and held a big position at a billion-dollar company. And yet today he'd smiled as he remembered his own student days in tiny lodgings. He hadn't been born rich. He'd come to see her to make sure she was all right.

And he'd fought for her—something no one had done before. Ever. A warm feeling expanded through her chest. "I don't know what to say. Thank you for the support. It means a lot."

Phillipe's shoulders relaxed and he took another drink of coffee. "I'm glad you're not really sick. You'll be back tomorrow?"

"You're sure this is okay? I have no desire to put you in a bad position with your boss."

"No worries about that. I promise."

She finished her coffee and put the cup down on a tiny table. "I appreciate you stopping by. I really do." She was even more glad he'd spoken of giving her a reference if—no, when—she left. She had to start looking toward her future. One that didn't include a position at Aurora Inc. Because even when the DNA test proved that she was Cedric's daughter, it was clear the family wanted nothing to do with her. Phillipe seemed to think differently, but she wouldn't get her hopes up. Phillipe hadn't seen the anger in Charlotte's eyes.

Which just meant her initial reasons for keeping the secret were completely valid. And it wasn't like she even blamed them for their response. She just felt...alone. Though a little less now, with Phillipe on her side.

"You all right, Annie?" Phillipe's concerned voice broke through her thoughts, and she looked up to find his startling blue eyes gazing into hers. Her stomach did that little flip again and she told it to go away. Phillipe had put his neck out for her. The last thing she needed to do was act like a ninny with a crush, even if it was true. She'd be lying if she didn't admit that one of the reasons she'd hated to leave her job was because she'd miss seeing him every day.

"I'm okay," she said softly. "This week has been a lot. Lots of drama. I'm not used to that."

He smiled a little and nodded. "This business, and this family? Drama happens. I try to ignore it and keep my part of the ship steady."

"And I appreciate that," Annie replied, giving a light laugh. "I promise, Phillipe, that I'll do whatever I can to make sure this situation doesn't affect my work or the launch. I know how important it is to you."

The light in his eyes dimmed for a moment, but then it was back again, and Annie wondered if she'd only been imagining it. He looked at her over the rim of his cup as he finished his coffee, then put his cup on the table next to hers. "Well, good. I should be going now. Thank you for the coffee. I'm so glad you're not really sick. I don't think we could do this launch without you."

He really shouldn't say things like that. He couldn't know how much someone like her took it to heart. Annie was self-aware enough to know that she needed to be needed, and right now, other than Phillipe, there wasn't a soul in the world who needed her one bit.

She got up and so did he, and she held out her hand, determined to keep things businesslike. "I'll see you tomorrow, eight sharp," she said briskly, smiling her best employee smile.

He took her hand and shook it but held it just a smidge too long, and his long fingers seemed to cling to hers just a little bit as he withdrew.

"À demain," he said quietly, and she resolved not to get all swoony, though it was difficult when he spoke French. He made everything sound so soft and lyrical.

Heavens, she really was a prize idiot for letting him get to her like this.

She walked him to the door and said goodbye, then shut the door behind him and rested her forehead against it. One week. She had one week left of pretending she didn't think her boss was sex on a stick. One week to come up with a new plan.

She turned away from the door and went to find her tiny laptop. It was time to polish up her résumé and start sending it out. As she sat on the little sofa again, she looked around the cramped flat and felt a wave of sadness wash over her. It was tiny with no closet space and a miniscule kitchen, but it was hers, and it was in Paris, and she was going to miss it all horribly.

Then she rolled her shoulders and lifted her chin. There was no point in feeling sorry for herself.

CHAPTER FOUR

ANNIE WALKED BACK into the office carrying her favorite travel mug full of coffee, as she planned to keep it replenished. She'd missed a whole afternoon of work, and time was of the essence with the details of the launch.

There were some odd looks cast her way, but she just offered a smile and a greeting and nothing else as she took her position behind her desk and clipped the earpiece for the phone to her ear. With a relieved sigh—it was so good to be back—she booted up her computer and went to log in.

"It's not even eight."

She looked up to see Phillipe smiling down on her, his eyes warm. "I'm a few minutes early. I figure my situation is already tenuous without adding tardiness to my list of faults."

"When will you have the results?" he asked.

"I don't know. A few days? A week, maybe?" She shrugged. "When you're Aurora Pemberton, you can pay to have these things expedited." She sat back in her chair a bit. "Right now, I have a more pressing problem. The catering menu is to be finalized by ten this morning and I have a list of tasks a mile long. Who knew that missing an afternoon would create such a backlog?"

Phillipe frowned. "Do you need a coffee?"

She lifted her travel mug. "Already on it."

His smile was a sexy curve of his lips and flash of teeth, and it lit his face. Goodness, she liked that she'd put that grin there. There wasn't much about him she didn't like.

One week.

"Let me know if you need anything. I can loan you Lisette for the day if that would help." Lisette was his executive assistant, pretty and quiet and efficient. And she had her own workload.

"Thank you. I'll let you know, but if I start now, I should be able to get caught up."

"Anything you need," he replied, his gaze touching hers.

You, she thought, but she wouldn't say it in a million years. Her crush was rapidly turning into more after the consideration he'd shown the past few days.

He disappeared into his office. She looked up to realize that a few curious stares were turned in her direction. It really was strange being in more of an open concept for admin in the department. She was sure her coworkers were wondering why she'd been gone yesterday, and why Phillipe had gone straight to her desk this morning.

Rather than engage—what could she say, after all—she logged in and brought up her project management software.

She'd only been logged in for five minutes when an urgent email notification popped up from a coworker in the PR department who was helping with the launch details. An issue had come up with on-site security and she couldn't find the guest list to confirm attendance.

Annie sighed. She responded asking if they could have a quick meeting to go over particulars and make sure nothing had slipped through the cracks. Ten minutes later she was on a different floor, walking into Claudine's small office.

"You are a sight for sore eyes," Claudine said, grinning up at her. "I got worried when you went out sick yesterday. You're feeling all right now?"

"I'm fine." Annie pulled out a chair and prepared to get to work. She wished she could talk about what was going on with someone other than Phillipe. She'd considered calling Rachael in Norwich, just as a sounding board, but something had held her back. Rachael was the only other person in her world who knew she was Cedric's daughter. She'd also warned Annie against the scheme of working in Paris, worried it would backfire. Now that it had, Annie figured she just wasn't up for a conversation of *I told you so.* She liked Claudine very much, but this was too big, too incendiary. So she kept her mouth shut.

They spent the next ninety minutes going through the guest list and then coming up with a contingency plan for security, since so many VIPs were going to be attending. Claudine was overseeing press releases and then official coverage of the event for Aurora; together they arranged for the press passes that would be needed for the night. Annie didn't recognize many of the names, but she certainly knew the magazines and media outlets they represented. It was hard not to be a little starstruck about it all. It was also a lot of pressure to get things right. She wasn't used to being a cog in a wheel this big.

"Is catering set?" Claudine asked, finally sitting back in her chair.

"I sent the approved lists back this morning, so we should be good there." Thank God she didn't have to organize every detail; mostly it was coordinating and arranging approvals. "I'm nervous about this, Claudine. I've never done something this big before."

Claudine flapped a hand. "You've done fine."

"But I'm out of my comfort zone—"

"Don't be silly," Claudine interrupted. "Maybe this is bigger, grander than you're used to. But what the position needed was someone with great organizational skills, and you've got those in abundance."

Annie appreciated the vote of confidence, but her mind slipped back to Bella and the rest of the family. Would they think the same? Did they care about her organizational skills? And what about Phillipe? He'd put himself smack in the middle. If things didn't end well, how would his career be affected because he'd championed her?

The days passed all too quickly in a haze of planning and preparation. Annie had just solved the security issue when there was a problem with the main display that was to be center stage. Five names were added to the guest list and the press list finalized. Annie was both exhausted and energized. The event promised to be a who's who of entertainment and fashion, and she was the one putting it together. Did she feel out of her league? Definitely. Was she pulling it off anyway? Yes. Because she was smart and capable. For the first time, she'd been given the opportunity to show just how much. And the stakes were high, too. The last thing she wanted to do was fail in front of the Pembertons—or worse, let Phillipe down.

She was in a meeting with him in his office when his phone buzzed. He looked down and frowned. "It's William," he said, and picked it up.

"Yes…yes, of course. Right away."

He hung up and met her gaze.

"What's wrong?" she asked. He'd gone still, and there was a look of sympathy in his eyes that put her on edge.

"William was looking for you. The family wants to see you upstairs. In Bella's office."

Her fingers started to tremble. She'd known this moment was coming. She was confident in the results. Her mum wouldn't have lied. So why was she so nervous? Why was she afraid to hear the results? What difference could it possibly make to her?

"I'm going with you," Phillipe said, rising from his chair once again. "You're not going into this alone."

She nodded dumbly and stood, feeling a bit shaky. "I should say no, but I'd be glad of the moral support."

"You're no good to me if you faint," he replied, his tone dry, and she started to laugh. She could always rely on his subtle sarcasm and dry wit. It was quite charming, really. He seemed to know just how to ease the tension in situations with a little quip. How could he not see that in himself? The jest helped her settle her nerves, too. She was going to walk into Bella's office with her head held high.

"Let's leave that here," he said, taking the file folder from her hands and putting it on the desk. "Ready?"

"No," she said, "but I have to face this head-on. It's the only way I'll be able to move forward, whatever that looks like."

They went together to the elevators and up to the fifth floor. Annie's heart pounded against her ribs, anxiety ratcheting up her pulse and making her slightly light-headed, though she was determined not to show it. Phillipe was steady and solid beside her, and she was so grateful for his presence. He tapped on Bella's door—the expansive office for the CEO that had windows overlooking the Seine—and they stepped inside.

The Paris-based members of the family were already present: Bella, Stephen, William, Christophe. Annie took a breath and faced them head-on. "Will Aurora and Charlotte be joining us?"

Stephen shook his head. "No. We spoke to them already this morning."

She couldn't read his expression. Stephen, she realized, had a heck of a poker face.

"Phillipe," William said, his tone low and serious. "This is a family matter."

"I asked him to join me," Annie said quickly, quite willing to take the blame rather than put Phillipe in the middle any more than he already was. "To...to be a witness."

"For heaven's sake," Bella said, and she came around her desk. "Stephen, you don't have to look so intimidating. And Annie, you are fully within your rights to want to have someone with you. Everyone calm down."

Stephen's expression tightened, but he said nothing, letting Bella take the lead.

Bella smiled a little, though it wasn't exactly warm. It wasn't hostile, either. It was...sad, if Annie had to hazard a guess. Her presence here was not good news, no matter what the outcome. She'd caused this family pain, and she didn't like that one bit.

"Anemone, we asked you up here today because the test results are in. Your sample was tested against mine. And it seems we are, indeed, half-sisters."

CHAPTER FIVE

ANNIE WASN'T QUITE prepared for the relief that rushed through her at the official confirmation. She stared at Bella for a stunned moment and became aware of Phillipe's strong hand on her shoulder. "All right?" he asked, his voice low.

She gave a quick nod. William and Stephen looked grim, Christophe seemed intrigued with the whole thing, and Bella was looking at her with something like sympathy etched on her features. "I'm sorry," Annie said quietly. "I never wanted any of this. Never wanted to hurt you or your family."

"That's already done," Stephen said. "But if you mean that you don't want to harm our family any further, we're having papers prepared by legal for you to sign."

She frowned. "What sort of papers?"

William spoke up. "A deal that will ensure this information won't get out. Basically, you'll be paid for your silence."

Anger began to flicker in Annie's gut, tiny flames of resentment that the people she'd come to know and even like over the past months were not above simply paying someone off to be quiet. "How much?" she asked.

Fire flashed in Stephen's eyes. "Ah. Now we get to it."

Bella was the one who spoke. "Five million euros."

Annie's mouth dropped open. Phillipe's hand slid off her shoulder. Five million euros… What would she ever do with that much money? Hush money. Money to be someone other than who she really was. She shook her head. "I don't want it. I don't want any money."

Stephen snorted, then looked her dead in the eye. "How much will it take?"

They didn't believe her. It suddenly dawned on her that this was the life they led, wasn't it? People always wanting something, whether it was riding on coattails or money to keep a secret. Everyone's motives were suspect. How sad. At times, Annie had hated their small flat and modest car compared with so many other schoolmates. Now she wouldn't trade it for this type of existence for anything in the world.

"I understand you completely," she said, cold certainty settling over her. "I even understand why. I'm your father's dirty little secret and you don't want it to get out. But I don't want money. I don't want anything. I'll finish up my work tomorrow and you won't have to worry about seeing me again."

Silence dropped over the room. Even Stephen's face had softened with surprise. She turned to leave.

"Anemone," Bella whispered, a note of entreaty in her voice.

"Leave her be," Stephen said, but his voice had gentled the tiniest bit. Perhaps she'd finally gotten through to the implacable earl that she was not a gold digger.

William and Christophe said nothing.

"Go downstairs." Phillipe's soft voice was kind and reassuring. "I'll meet you there in a moment."

She nodded dumbly and left the room. She walked to the stairs, needing to keep moving rather than waiting for the elevator. She got to her floor and went directly to Phillipe's office, and then started to pace as she worked through what had just happened.

She was Cedric's daughter for sure. His family hated her. They wanted to pay her off.

She could take the money and then she'd never have to worry again. Of course, there would be the small matter of her pride and self-respect. At this point, it was all she had left. And she would rather make her own way than do it by denying her own existence. Oh, she'd never sell the story or anything like that, but neither would she profit off her silence. She'd give it with her chin up and head held high.

Two more days. Two more and the launch would be over, and she would no longer work for Aurora Inc.

And she'd no longer have a reason to see Phillipe each day.

Phillipe stood in the doorway to Bella's office. In all the months he'd been at Aurora's head office, he'd never been this nervous. But maybe that was because what he wanted to say had nothing to do with fragrance or business but everything to do with the woman who'd just walked away, looking as if the world had just dropped out from beneath her feet.

He looked at William, the family member he was most familiar with. "You might have been a little gentler with her," he said, his voice tight.

"Why?" Stephen answered ahead of William, and it annoyed Phillipe. Stephen was the Earl of Chatsworth, and he could be a good sort, but he could also be a bit cold and unfeeling. Phillipe understood that he was the oldest and that he was just trying to protect his family, but Annie *was* his family now. And he'd treated her contemptuously.

Phillipe had known boys like Stephen his whole life: entitled, powerful, never questioning their place in the world. It had angered him then, and it angered him now. He looked the earl right in the eye. "Because she is your half-sister. Because she has not once shown any desire to hurt you or your family. Because you grew up with your father and she will never know him. And because it is never a bad thing to show a little compassion."

Stephen's eyes widened, and he had the grace to look a bit embarrassed.

To Phillipe's surprise, it was Christophe who spoke up.

"Leroux is right, or at least partly right. I am not as closely related to you as Anemone is, yet I was brought up in your house and given every advantage, including that of a big family of siblings. It is not her fault she was conceived, nor is it her fault she was kept a secret."

Stephen cut in. "But if news of this got out…"

"Then what?" Bella stepped forward, twisting her hands together. "Then the world would know that our father was not the paragon we made him out to be. And Maman would be the woman who'd been cheated on. Yes, there'd be scandal. But it wouldn't be the first time this family was embroiled in one." She looked at Stephen and William. "It wasn't that long ago that you both brought scandal to the door, and we didn't disown you."

Phillipe had remained quiet because it seemed the siblings had some differing opinions that were worth hearing. But he stepped in again, calling himself a fool for getting involved, but knowing Anemone deserved better.

"She has not asked for any money. And believe me, she could use it. She lives in a tiny little flat and takes transit everywhere… The woman is on a tight budget. You offered her money to go away just now, rather than offering her a place in your family. I honestly thought this family was more generous, but perhaps I was wrong."

"Now, Phillipe," William began.

"I'm sorry. I know I've overstepped, and this is a family matter, but Anemone has been nothing but mature and composed throughout this whole launch project. She's far stronger than people realize, actually." He shoved his hands in his pockets. "I'll be going now, but I needed to stand up for her. Someone has to. I'm not sure anyone has in her whole life."

He left the office with his heart pounding. If he felt like an imposter in his job position, he'd certainly overstepped the mark insinuating himself into a Pemberton family situation. But he felt what he'd said strongly: the more he got to know Annie, the more he realized that no one had stood up for her. As Cedric Pemberton's daughter, she should have had access to opportunities. Instead she'd been hidden away as if she wasn't worth knowing.

Well, she was. He hadn't been able to stop thinking about her, for example.

He found her in his office, pacing the floor, eyes dry now but her lips set in a firm line. She was still angry. Good. She should be.

"They wanted to pay me off. Give me money to go away! I mean, I didn't expect them to greet me with outstretched arms of welcome or anything, but this... Oh, I'm so insulted."

She was beautiful all fired up like this. Her eyes were like blue sparks and her cheeks had a pink flush to them. The more he got to know her, the more he realized how strong she was.

"What would you like me to do? How can I help?" he found himself asking.

She halted her pacing and stared at him. "Oh." For a moment, she looked nonplussed, as if his question was such a surprise that she'd forgotten what she was about. "Phillipe, you've already done too much. You fought for me to keep my job last week, and listened to me, and went with me today. You went far and above what a boss would normally do."

"I'd like to think that by now I'm not just your boss." At her continued confusion, he added, "I'd like to think we're friends."

Friends. That sounded so mundane and didn't reflect his feelings at all. It was, however, the safest and easiest descriptor. For she couldn't be anything more, could she?

"I…um…well…" She seemed flustered as she looked at him.

Phillipe momentarily felt foolish. "Are we not?"

"I just… Well, I didn't expect it, is all. You've been very supportive. And I could use a friend." She started blinking rapidly and then gave her shoulders a shake and cleared her throat. "I'm not going to cry about this. I'm not. It won't help anything."

"You're disappointed."

"Very. I don't know what I expected, but it wasn't Stephen's coldness. It was so calculating."

Phillipe weighed what to say next, finally deciding on: "We talked briefly after you left. Not everyone feels as strongly as Stephen, you know. You might find you have a few allies in the bunch. If you give them time—"

She scoffed. "I doubt it. When push comes

to shove, they'll stick together against me, the outsider. I was foolish to even come here." She looked into Phillipe's eyes. "I wish I'd never found out Cedric was my father. I could have just carried on with my life."

He understood the wishing thing. He'd often had the same thoughts about his marriage, wishing he'd never married Madelyn, wondering where he'd be if he hadn't. But that wasn't the reality they lived in, was it? And he said so.

"Well, you can't change it now. All you can do is decide how you want to move forward." He went to her and picked up her hands. "You would have wondered who your father was forever. And if you hadn't come here, you always would have wondered about the family. Now you know. Now you can put those questions behind you and move forward." The truth struck him as he said the words. "The same way I must. I'll be honest, Annie. I haven't been able to move past my divorce, but the truth is I have my answers and I'm still stuck. I'd like to stop being that way somehow."

A small smile flickered on Annie's lips. "What a sad pair we are, Phillipe."

He smiled back, and suddenly the room was warm again and to his surprise Annie was in his arms, giving him a hug.

His arms came around her and tightened. She

felt so good, so right. The scent of her hair was slightly floral and soft tendrils tickled his jaw where she was tucked against him. It would take very little to shift, to put his finger beneath her chin and have her look up at him, to focus on her berry-ripe lips before kissing her...

"What is this for?" he asked softly, rubbing a hand over her back. He didn't want to let her go. He didn't even care that he was technically still her boss. She had less than two days left of work. All too soon he wouldn't be her boss and he wouldn't see her at all. The thought made him feel hollow and lonely. He was going to miss her smile, her energy, her everything.

"Because you've stood up for me through all of this. And because that's the first time you've really opened up about yourself."

"I won't let it happen again."

She pulled back a little and treated him to a teasing smile. "Are you sure?"

He nodded. "Actually, yes, because we have a launch to finalize and attend. Both of us."

She slid out of his embrace and the smile on her face fell away. "Me, there? Oh, the family isn't going to want me there, Phillipe. They want me gone and invisible as soon as possible. My presence at the launch is a no-go."

"You did promise," he said. And he truly had meant what he'd said days ago about the moral support. Not in any romantic sense, but having an ally in the room so he didn't have to go through the evening alone. He wasn't good at the mingling thing.

"Well, that was before. You can't hold me to it now." She started pacing again. "When Friday afternoon arrives, and the day's work is done, I'm no longer an Aurora Inc. employee."

"Then go as my plus-one. I am allowed one, you know."

He wasn't sure where the invitation came from. To ask her not as a colleague but as a date. But he'd done it now and he liked the idea. "You've put in so much work. This way you get to admire the fruits of your labors. Drink champagne. Nibble on whatever delicacies are being circulated."

"And feel daggers in my back every time one of the Pembertons sees me? No thanks."

"Please, don't paint them all with Stephen's brush. Christophe understands. And I think Bella likes you. Please, Annie."

But she shook her head. "I can't, Phillipe. I'm sorry. I know I owe you for all your support, but I can't go to the launch. Not after today. I'll be home, making decisions about where my life is to go next."

"You'll stay in Paris," he said, as if it were a foregone conclusion.

"Maybe, but not necessarily. There's nothing holding me here. And nothing waiting for me back home, either. The world is my oyster, as they say. Which makes my decision harder rather than easier."

Nothing holding her here. Of course not.

"Thank you for going with me earlier. I truly appreciate it." She tucked a wayward strand of hair behind her ear. "But now I should get back to work. There's very little time left and still work to be done."

He let her go because he didn't know what else to say. He cared for her, didn't want her to go, but he couldn't identify what it was he wanted from her. Friendship? Perhaps. He had few friends in Paris. And at times he wanted more, but was he ready to give more? Did he want to see her socially, as in dating? To what end? He wasn't looking to get married ever again. Having his heart stomped on once was bad enough. And he certainly didn't want to have a fling. She didn't seem like the fling type. More like the get-attached type, and that just resulted in people being hurt.

No, it was better to let her go. He'd become far too involved as it was. In two days she'd be gone, the launch would be over, and life would go back to what it used to be around here.

It sounded positively horrible.

* * *

Annie grabbed her purse from a desk drawer and once more looked around the office. For the second time in a week, she was leaving, only this time she wouldn't be returning. She was leaving more than a job behind. She was leaving the only blood family she had in the world, and they wanted nothing to do with her. It felt like an ending in so many ways, and not the happy ending she'd always dreamed.

Time to find a job. Start over. It sounded like such a huge undertaking.

She was halfway to the elevators when she heard her name being called. "Anemone? Annie!"

She spun around and saw Lisette rushing toward her. "Oh, good," Lisette said, reaching her. "I caught you before you left. Come with me."

"I'm sorry?" Annie asked, confused. Could she not just leave with a minimum of fuss and put this all behind her?

"We don't have much time. Come with me." She put her hand on Annie's arm, but when Annie resisted, Lisette halted, looked into Annie's face and smiled. "He said you would resist."

"Who did?"

"Phillipe. The launch is in under four hours. We have to find you a dress and shoes and get your hair done."

Annie shook her head. "I'm not going to the launch. I've just finished my last day and I'm going home." And she was going to order in some dinner and drink an obscene amount of wine and feel sorry for herself, and tomorrow she would get up and call her best friend and then start making plans.

"He said you would say that, too. I was shocked to hear you are leaving. When he asked me to see to this, I agreed right away. Come on. There's no time to waste."

Annie trotted after her, not because she had changed her mind about going to the launch, but because Lisette was a lovely woman and Phillipe's executive assistant...and she was already walking away.

"Where are we going?" she asked, hurrying to catch up.

Lisette turned her head and flashed a smile. "Heaven," she replied. They went down two flights of stairs and then Lisette swiped a key card and led her through a set of glass doors into what looked like a miniature Aurora boutique, right here in the head office building.

Annie halted. "Okay, so I knew this was here...in theory."

"There aren't many offices on the second floor. No need for most of the staff to be here. But it does mean we can pluck an item from the season's designs at a moment's notice if needed for an event or publicity opportunity."

As Annie looked around, she realized that it wasn't quite like a shop; the racks were organized in a far more utilitarian fashion and there were no flashy decorations. Just racks of clothes, shelves of accessories, and great lighting.

"All right. You need a gown."

"Lisette, I appreciate this, but I can't go. Besides, what will the Pembertons do when I show up in an Aurora design?"

Lisette grinned. "Hopefully realize how good it looks on you. Listen, Phillipe is a wonderful man. We both know this. And I can tell he cares for you. I don't know why you're leaving, but if he wants you at this event—an event you planned, by the way—I'm going to get you there." She played her last card. "Neither of us wants to disappoint Phillipe Leroux."

Lisette had her there. She was terrified of facing the Pembertons but the idea of walking in there tonight and seeing Phillipe in his tuxedo, meeting him dressed in couture... It was so very tempting.

"I don't even know what would look good," she said weakly.

"Hmm." Lisette looked her up and down. "I

think I have just the dress. It's last year's line, but I think it'd be perfect."

Annie sighed in frustration. "Did you not hear me say I am not going?"

"I heard you." Lisette came over and took her hands, a gesture that was shocking and lovely all at once. "Look, Annie. I've spent over ten years working for Aurora and the last eighteen months for Phillipe. He is the best boss I have ever had. When he first came here, he was in over his head and there was this... I don't know. Sadness about him. But lately... He smiles more. I think you have something to do with that. If this is really your last day, why not take a chance and show up at the hotel and knock his eyeballs out? He's right. You've worked so hard, and you should be there. And it means so much to him that he planned this whole surprise for you. You should be there to support each other. Don't let him down."

Heat rushed to Annie's cheeks. The one sure way to get to her was through Phillipe. Though, supporting each other...the tone of that was slightly different from that of boss and employee. *Friends*, he'd said. Oh, she was so confused. She didn't know how to define their relationship. Even the word *relationship* seemed presumptuous.

She wasn't actually thinking of going along with this, was she?

Lisette went to a rack, sorted through a few items and pulled out a stunning black-and-white gown. "This is the one. Try it on. I think it'll suit your figure perfectly."

Annie reached out and touched a single finger to the fine fabric. The trouble was she wanted to accept. She wanted to go and see the results of her hard work. She wanted to walk in the door and find Phillipe and see his eyes widen when he saw her in an Aurora original. It was probably the wrong motivation, but it was there just the same, tempting her.

"There's a changing area back here." Lisette took her hand and led her toward the back of the room where a few curtained areas were set up. "I'll be back in a moment."

The dress was fancier than anything Annie had ever laid eyes on before. The white bodice was strapless but had a halter overlay of chiffon. The high waist gave way to a long, slender fall of black silk under more chiffon. She shimmied out of her clothes and slid into the dress. The built-in bra cupped her breasts perfectly, and the zipper was a tiny bit snug, but she could still get it to the top.

She looked down. The dress was at least an inch, maybe two, too long.

Disappointment washed over her. Lisette had picked the perfect dress in the perfect size, a testament to her experience and keen eye. But Annie couldn't do anything about her height.

"How is it?" Lisette asked.

"Too long."

"Come out and let me see."

Annie shifted the curtain and stepped out. Directly across from the changeroom was a mirrored wall, and she caught her breath when she saw the dress. Oh, goodness. Was this really her?

"It's perfect. What size are your feet? A good pair of heels and that length will be just right."

Annie gathered up the skirt and followed Lisette into what appeared to be a huge closet. Inside, the walls were covered with racks of shoes. "Do you like closed heel or open? A sandal or a platform pump?"

"I have narrow heels. I actually like sandals or slingbacks. The strap keeps my heel secure instead of sliding out of the back of a pump."

"I know just the one. There's a pair of Louboutins in here that you'll love."

Louboutins. She could pay rent for a few months for the cost of a pair of those. Was this even real?

Lisette ran her finger along a shelf until she found the shoes she wanted. "Here, try these."

The slingbacks had an open toe with a pretty curve pattern bordered by glittering rhinestones. The heel strap was also adorned by the rhinestones, adding some serious bling to the classic design.

"Step into these," Lisette said, kneeling before her.

The fit was lovely, and Annie turned her foot this way and that, watching the stones sparkle. "This is too much. I can't do this."

Lisette looked up at her. "You can." She stood and looked Annie in the eye. "Anemone, I want to tell you something. Please, sit here for a moment." She led her to a soft settee, where they both perched on the stuffed cushions.

"When Phillipe first came here from Grasse, it wasn't all... How is it you say it? Smooth sailing." She smiled. "There was definitely an adjustment for him in his role with the company, but more than that, he was miserable. It took a while for him to be comfortable with me. Oh, we got along fine working together, but there was nothing personal. Until I put through a call one day and afterward I could tell he was upset. He shared with me then that it had been his ex-wife."

Annie nodded as Lisette patted her hand. "I am divorced as well, and I told him so, and while Phillipe never shared very much, I certainly understood why he was struggling. After a while he relaxed, smiled more, grew more confident. But I have never seen him smile as much as he does when you're around. He's... lighter somehow. And maybe there is absolutely nothing between you, and I certainly don't want to suggest there's anything inappropriate. But he wants this for you, and I think you should put on this dress and shoes and get your hair done and go to the launch. He needs you."

The speech was making a lump form in Annie's throat. It was difficult to think of Phillipe being less than his charming self, to be in so much pain that the cheeky smile and dancing eyes she knew didn't exist.

"I don't know what to say."

"Say you'll go. And don't tell him I told you any of this." She laughed a little. "He's a private man, and a good one." Lisette put her hands together. "All right. There's no time to waste. The dress and shoes are sorted. Now you just need jewelry." She reached into her bag and took out a small rectangular box embossed with the Aurora logo.

"I can't. It's too much."

"You can. Open it."

Annie shook her head and let out a breath, feeling far too much like Cinderella with Lisette as her fairy godmother, even if it was at Phillipe's instruction. She took the box and slid off the lid. Inside was couched a delicate gold necklace, with a gossamer fine chain and a pendant in the shape of a bee sipping from a flower. "Nectar," she said softly, taking the necklace out of the box.

"Most appropriate, don't you think?" Lisette took the chain and hooked it at the nape of Annie's neck. "There. In exactly ten minutes, a car is going to take you to an appointment for a mani-pedi, plus makeup and hair. It's going to be a tight squeeze, so the car will wait for you. The driver will deliver you to the hotel. Okay?"

"You're officially my fairy godmother," Annie remarked, and offered Lisette a genuine smile. "I feel like everything will disappear at the stroke of midnight."

"Don't let it." Lisette squeezed her hand. "When you find something worth holding on to, don't let it go. Now, let's get this dress into a garment bag for you and get you to your car."

She changed quickly and before long she was at the front entrance just as the car service pulled up. Lisette pulled her in for a quick hug. "Good luck," she said, smiling.

Annie slid into the car and perched on the soft leather seat. Nerves settled low in her belly. Phillipe had gone to all the bother to arrange all of this—for her. She was going to the launch. And her entire family was going to be there.

As the car made its way to whatever appointment she had next, Annie made a decision. Tonight she would hold her head high. She was a Pemberton, too, and she'd act like it. Maybe she was leaving Aurora Inc., but she was leaving with her pride and self-respect intact.

And tonight she would live up to Phillipe's faith in her.

CHAPTER SIX

THE DOORWAY TO the ballroom was less than fifty feet away, but Annie couldn't seem to go any farther. Nerves were making her nearly ill, and she ran a hand over the soft fabric at her waist. She'd spent two hours having her hair, makeup and nails done, and the results had blown her away. Her eyes seemed bigger, lips plumper, and her sandy-blond hair was piled on top of her head in an oversize topknot anchored with a braid. She was horribly afraid something would let go and her hair would come cascading down in a poufy mess, even though the stylist had assured her that would not happen.

The hall was quiet, while the sounds of music and voices were muffled through the ornate doors to the venue.

"Bonsoir, mademoiselle," a voice said, and she realized it was a member of staff waiting to open the ballroom doors.

"Bonsoir," she replied breathlessly, her chest

cramping. She hadn't thought before about the anxiety that came from entering a room alone—a room in which she knew barely anyone. This dress, her entire appearance—it wasn't her. She was the kind of woman who was normally found behind the bar or behind the scenes holding some sort of clipboard. Not tonight. All because Phillipe and Lisette had decided she was Cinderella.

A deep breath. *I am a Pemberton*, she reminded herself. She stopped fussing with her skirt and gave a nod. It was now or never.

The door was opened, and she stepped through.

The voices and music were much louder once the doors were open. The ballroom was simply stunning, just as she'd imagined it, like a spring garden brought inside. White linens graced the tables, and arrangements of spring flowers were everywhere: pink ranunculus, grape hyacinth, creamy-white rosebuds; rainbows of tulips, delicate orchids, fragrant peonies and, of course, irises. The delicate profusion of color made the room a veritable bower, while a platform at the front—an empty beehive—showcased the new fragrance, Nectar.

And about ten feet away from the dais was Phillipe.

It was as if he could sense her gaze on him, as

his eyes flicked up and saw her standing there. There was a moment of confusion, then recognition, then a smile so wide that her heart started fluttering. She had to move. She couldn't stand in one spot for the whole night. So she let out a breath, prayed she didn't trip on the mile-high heels and made her way across the room.

Without breaking eye contact, he excused himself from his companion and gave her his full attention, so that when she finally stopped in front of him, it was as if they were the only two people in the world.

"I didn't think you'd come." His voice was low and smooth, sliding along her nerve endings. *Oh, dear.*

"I wasn't going to," she admitted. "Not after what happened." She smiled and plucked at her dress a little self-consciously. "But you had Lisette play fairy godmother. I couldn't refuse."

His eyes shone. "You look... My word, Anemone. Nothing I can come up with is adequate. Ravishing."

She hoped she wasn't blushing. She clasped her fingers together and licked her lips. "I have never worn a dress like this in my life, Phillipe. It's an Aurora original. How did you... I mean..." It occurred to her that Phillipe had gone to a lot of trouble and expense to make this happen. She would never be able to pay him back.

"You deserve a night of glamour. You planned the event. It wouldn't be right if you weren't here to enjoy it." He offered his arm. "Come. Let's get some champagne and celebrate our victory tonight. All your hard work has paid off. This whole event is amazing."

She linked her arm with his, liking the feeling of the fine thread of his tuxedo sleeve beneath her hand. *Our victory*, he'd said, linking the two of them together. Her heart tripped at the thought before she reminded herself to keep her feet firmly on the ground. "I kind of wanted to have real bees in that hive, you know," she said.

He chuckled. "Of course you did."

"Phillipe… I don't know how I can ever repay you."

"No repayment necessary. I wanted to do this for you, Annie." He stopped and turned her to face him. "You belong here. Your family should have seen to it. You're a Pemberton and you made this whole event happen."

Still, nothing to do with him wanting her here, or anything…intimate, as Lisette had suggested.

"But this puts you in an awkward position at Aurora," she reminded him. "I don't want you to risk yourself just to prove a point or something. It's not worth it."

"Is it not?" His gaze delved into hers. "Perhaps I think it is."

One of the wait staff approached and offered them champagne. Once the flutes were in their hands, Phillipe offered a toast. "To Nectar," he said, touching his rim to hers. "And to you, for pulling this evening together."

"Just doing my job. Or at least, what was my job."

His smile faded a little as she sipped from her glass. "You're really done at Aurora, then? You're not going to fight for your position?"

She nodded. "I'm done. I won't beg, either for my job or for acceptance. I'm better off alone than scrounging for scraps. Thanks to you, I'm leaving with a good reference, and once the clock strikes midnight tonight, I'll be searching the help-wanted ads." She fought to keep her voice cheerful. "A whole new beginning."

He took a drink of his champagne. "You don't sound that sorry. Is this a good thing?"

She reached out and touched his arm. "Phillipe, I have loved working at Aurora and the last few months. It's been amazing. But on a personal level, with the family, it's too complicated. It was a foolish plan from the start."

"I'll miss you."

Her pulse fluttered as his eyes were steady on hers. "I will miss you, too. More than I can say."

Someone laughed nearby and diverted their attention for a few moments; when they looked back at each other, there was something new in Phillipe's expression. "You know," he said, "this does mean I'm not your boss anymore."

"Oh." She took a quick drink of champagne, finishing the glass. Many of her feelings and thoughts where he was concerned had been inappropriate. Not so much anymore, if he wasn't her boss.

"Maybe we could go for coffee sometime. Or dinner. I don't have many friends in Paris, you know." His eyebrow did a slight shift, and she thought she caught a glimpse of a little dimple. He really was too charming.

"That might be nice," she murmured, and when another server came near, she swapped out her empty glass for a full one. Across the room, she saw William and Gabi talking to Charlotte and her husband, Jacob. William looked up and saw her and his eyebrows lifted in shock. Charlotte followed his gaze and her expression darkened.

"I've been spotted," she murmured.

"Ah yes. But don't worry, there won't be a scene," he said. "They wouldn't chance it. Don't get me wrong, I'm so very glad you're here. But

I expect it might feel a little like walking into the lion's den, *oui*?"

She gave a shaky laugh. *"Exactement,"* she replied, then forced a smile.

"You are dressed for battle, though," he replied. "My trust in Lisette was not misplaced."

"She was very persistent. She's a good assistant, Phillipe. You're lucky to have her."

He nodded. "She is. After my divorce I'm afraid I was not very fun to work for. But Lisette had been through it after her first marriage, and she was steady as a rock."

"You don't talk about that much," Annie observed.

"For a long time, I stewed in my anger. Lately, though, I've been thinking about what happened. Madelyn had an affair, and there's no question that was wrong. But she was also married to a man who was a workaholic. I put everything I had into the lab. It was my passion. Coupled with my need to prove myself, I think I spent more time trying to be what I thought she wanted rather than who she needed."

"And she found that somewhere else."

He nodded. "It's hard to forgive. I'm not sure I ever will. Anyway, it's over and done, and now I'm in Paris, at this amazing event, with the most beautiful woman in the room on my arm."

"Phillipe," she murmured, her cheeks heating.

"You *are* beautiful," he assured her. "And since I'm no longer your boss, perhaps it is all right for me to say so?"

She nodded, flustered but enjoying his compliments.

Phillipe stopped and introduced Annie to a colleague from another department, and as they were chatting, Annie glanced around and saw Bella staring at her. There wasn't exactly disapproval in her expression, but confusion, perhaps. Stephen joined his sister and when he glanced over, Annie felt the jolt of the eye contact to her toes. She felt like such an imposter.

They were moving on when Annie leaned over. "Bella and Stephen have seen me."

"Are you all right?"

"I'm not going to worry about it right now. I'm just going to stay out of their way."

"I will stay by your side," he promised.

"But you have obligations. Have you met with the press already?"

He led her closer to the perimeter of the room, away from the loudest of the conversations. "I've met with most of them. And completed my VIP obligations during the private cocktail hour before the event."

"You should circulate as the man of the hour," Annie insisted, pleased that he'd offered to remain with her, but knowing deep down she could not hide behind him all evening. "Go. I'll be fine. We'll catch up in a while."

"You're sure?"

"I'm sure."

With a squeeze of his hand on her arm and a reassuring smile, he moved away, taking some of Annie's confidence with him.

She circulated a little, mostly speaking to staff she recognized and a few guests, but she was too starstruck to approach many in attendance. She recognized probably half a dozen models, a few actors, and even a few reality TV stars. She was so out of her element here. The food looked amazing, but she was too nervous to eat and afraid she'd get something on the gorgeous dress, particularly the white bodice. Her feet hurt from the heels—she was unused to wearing ones this high and they were brand-new—and every time her attention was diverted, it seemed she turned back to find her champagne glass full again. That was dangerous, especially on an empty stomach. She put down her full glass and made her way to the powder room, stopping to grab a glass of club soda instead on her way back into the ballroom.

When she turned around, Bella was there.

The two women stared at each other for a prolonged moment, and then Annie spoke first. "Good evening, Bella."

"I'm surprised to see you here," Bella replied, not unkindly, but her tone wasn't overly warm, either.

"Phillipe insisted, since much of the planning for the event crossed my desk. It's going well, I think?"

"It is," Bella admitted. "You did do a good job, Anemone. Despite current…issues, I can't deny that."

"Thank you. I appreciate that."

Bella nodded at the dress as she accepted a drink from the bartender. "Last year's spring line, I think."

"That's what I was told. It's lovely. Beautiful and surprisingly comfortable."

"Phillipe again?"

Annie did not want to get Phillipe in any sort of trouble, but she could hardly lie and say she'd paid for it. Everyone knew she could not afford such a dress. "I couldn't attend wearing a little black dress off the rack," she finally said, giving a little shrug.

"Indeed not." Bella looked at her again until Annie felt rather like a bug in a jar. "Perhaps we should have seen to it. But you were so determined to not take any money."

"I truly don't want it." Annie stared at the wedge of lime floating in her glass. "This is my last Aurora event. After tonight I'll be out of your hair for good. You won't have to see me again. I came tonight as a favor to Phillipe, nothing more."

"He means a lot to you."

"He has been a wonderful boss and a good friend."

Bella turned to walk away but Annie called her back. "Bella?"

When Bella turned back around, Annie swallowed against the tightness in her throat before speaking. "Please, tell the others? Tell them that I never wanted to cause trouble, that I won't be bothering you again. And that I'm sorry for any hurt I caused."

Was it just the light, or were Bella's eyes suspiciously shiny? "I'll pass along your message."

Then her half-sister was gone, disappeared into the crowd of beautiful people, leaving Annie on the periphery of the room.

She heard her name and turned her head too quickly. Her vision was a little fuzzy until she focused on Phillipe again. But the blurry vision made her glad she'd switched to club soda. "The party is going well, don't you think?" She made her voice deceptively perky.

He nodded. "It seems so." He looked at her closely. "You were talking to Bella. How did it go?"

She squared her shoulders. "I think we made

our peace, actually, and now I can move on. I was living in a fantasy where I got to work at Aurora and hope that someday I'd be welcomed into the family fold because they already knew and liked me. It was silly and immature of me. I'm leaving on my own terms with my pride and self-respect intact." She gave a little snort and angled a glance at him. "Look at me, still growing up at twenty-nine."

He put his hand on her arm, his fingers strong and warm, and the contact sent a shiver down her body. "I'm older than that, and I feel like I grew up tonight, too. Talking about Madelyn got me thinking about some of my decisions over the last few years with a clearer head. Maybe we never stop growing up. It's kind of a lovely thought, actually. There's always something new to learn, some new wisdom."

She sighed. "Why do we cling so hard to the past, anyway?"

She thought he was going to answer, but they were interrupted by Bella taking the stage. "Ladies and gentlemen, welcome to the Aurora launch of our new, fabulous scent, Nectar." Clapping erupted for a few moments before she continued. "I simply couldn't let the evening slip away without mentioning a few key people in Nectar's development. As you are all aware, it's been a year of change at Aurora. My brothers, sister, cousin and I have all taken on increased roles at Aurora and have brought new and fresh ideas to the table, but there's also been a large learning curve for all of us. Thankfully we had the best of teachers—our mother, the wonderful Aurora Germain." More clapping. Aurora was back in London tonight, and not at the launch. Somehow Annie was glad of that. The last time they'd met, Aurora had revealed that she'd known about Anemone's existence for all these years. Annie had very mixed feelings about that.

"My brother William has taken over much of the cosmetics division, including the fragrance department, and he's done such a brilliant job. Expect more great things to come from him in the months to come." She offered a warm smile. "But most of all, I'd like to thank our executive manager of fragrance, Phillipe Leroux." She swept a hand in his direction, and all eyes in the room turned their way.

Phillipe gave a small smile and nod.

"Phillipe has been intimately involved with Nectar, not only as the manager of this department but because he was a designer in our Grasse lab before coming to corporate. Phillipe actually designed this scent himself—it was his last one before he moved up to managing the facility in Grasse, where he oversaw the next steps in production. And then he came to Paris, working with us at our headquarters, making William's job a little easier by bringing his expertise and intelligence to the role. Phillipe, I know this night is incredibly special to you, so congratulations on such a triumph. We're so very happy you're part of the Aurora team."

It was high praise from Bella, and Phillipe's cheeks flushed a little as the applause filled the room. But Bella wasn't done yet.

"I want to thank one more person tonight before we all go off to enjoy the music and food and drink again. The planning of tonight fell to one person, and she did an amazing job pulling it all together. Thank you, Anemone, for your hard work to make this event a success."

Anemone fought to school her features. Never had she expected any sort of thanks, let alone public gratitude. Her gaze darted to William, Charlotte and Stephen, and saw they were smiling faintly in what she recognized was a public polite face. Christophe was watching her with what looked like sympathy in his eyes, though she couldn't imagine why. Then she looked back at Bella and attempted to respond with the same polite smile. The recognition was nice, but she didn't trust it, no matter how well their last interaction had gone.

And that was it, wasn't it? She didn't trust any

of this. She needed to get away from it, from this world, from the torment she felt every time she thought of her blood family—half, anyway. She was here because she didn't want to be alone. But she quickly came to realize that a person could be utterly alone while surrounded by family. Family was not blood. At least not always.

"Now, everyone, enjoy the party!"

Bella stepped off the dais. Annie stepped aside as more people came to speak with Phillipe now that he'd been singled out. It was only half past ten and she was ready to leave the fairy tale behind. She didn't belong here. The acknowledgment had been nice and all, but even Phillipe was more in his element than she was. He looked so comfortable and debonair in his tux, one hand casually resting in his pocket as he chatted to a man who seemed vaguely familiar to her, though she couldn't quite place him.

Her stomach growled. She hadn't eaten since this morning. As gorgeous and amazing as this event was—she'd planned it, after all—she was exhausted from the long day and the emotional energy that had gone into her transformation and appearance at the launch. All she wanted to do now was go home and crawl under a blanket and eat takeaway Chinese food. Maybe with a movie on in the background.

Phillipe paused by her shoulder and leaned

in. "I'm nearly ready to get out of here. Wait for me in the lobby?"

She nodded automatically, then felt a whole new surge of butterflies as she realized this meant they were leaving together—and before the evening was officially over. What did it mean? Perhaps nothing. But she remembered how he'd said she wasn't his employee anymore and how beautiful she was... The line that they'd never crossed before suddenly didn't exist.

She subtly made her way toward the door, pausing occasionally if someone offered a greeting. At the door she was handed a small, beautiful bag of Aurora swag, which she automatically took before sliding out into the hallway. The air was cooler here and she took a deep, fortifying breath before walking down the hall toward the elevator that would take her down to the lobby. The hotel was the fanciest she'd ever been in. Soaring ceilings, rich fabrics, floors so shiny she could see her reflection. And flowers... always fresh flowers everywhere. Staff in livery waiting to open a door or press a button. The luxury, the wide-open spaces and unobtrusive assistance had a surprising claustrophobic effect on her. She needed to get out. Get somewhere where she could breathe again.

A doorman held open the door for her and

she prepared to step through when she heard her name being called. She made a half turn and saw Phillipe striding toward her, his brows pulled together. "Annie."

"Sorry," she said as soon as he arrived at her side. "I suddenly needed some air."

"It's all right."

"You're sure you want to leave already? This is your party, after all."

"I'm sure. I've had enough schmoozing and networking for a year." He led her out through the door into the soft Paris evening. "Annie, what Bella said..."

"It was generous of her, but the longer I was in the room, the smaller it seemed to become. Maybe I've been Cinderella for the night, but it's not real. The Pembertons do not want me as part of their family." Tears clogged her throat. "I have to move on. I have to. For my own mental health. I was so wrong to come to Paris in the first place."

"But if you hadn't, I never would have met you. And that would have been a shame."

He had to stop saying these sweet things. "I'm ready to go home and put on my pajamas and get back to real life."

He watched her for a long moment, then reached for her hand. "But it's not even midnight."

She smiled a little smile. Every time he touched her it sent little sparks firing off in her body and in her heart. "I'm not going to dash off and leave a glass slipper, if that's what you're thinking. Truly, I thought I'd order in a late dinner and just..." Her voice trailed off. And do what? Feel sorry for herself? Wish she wasn't alone? Start thinking about what came next? She had no job, no home to go to. Leaving the party tonight truly put a period at the end of her time at Aurora Inc.

"That sounds wonderful. Are you up for some company? Nectar has been launched. There's been champagne and speeches and swag and mingling and Nectar is on its own now. I haven't eaten, either. But I understand if you'd rather not. If you'd rather be alone."

She wanted to be with him so much she ached with it. Would it make things worse, spending time with him tonight? Or could she look at it as one last evening to enjoy his company?

"You're sure you don't want to stay?"

He squeezed her fingers. "I'm sure. It was a great evening. You truly put together a wonderful event, but I've had enough. We can order in, my treat. My way of saying thank you for all your hard work."

Her hard work. Just employer to employee, platonic and all about work. It was appropriate but disappointing. And yet he'd gone to the trouble to ensure she attended, to make her feel pampered and cared for. The mixed signals kept ping-ponging around. She should just go home, but she found herself not ready to say goodbye just yet. She gave a nod. "That might be nice. Apparently I have a car service." She smiled at him, teasing. "Looks like we have a ride."

She called for the car and as they waited, she took a deep breath, imprinting the moment on her memory. The city glittered around them, and she realized that she was going to miss Paris. She had loved living here, but unless she found another well-paying job, she couldn't afford to live here alone. She would have to say goodbye to it, and to the man on her arm. But not yet. Not tonight.

The car came to a stop in front of them. She slid into the back seat and then shifted so that Phillipe could climb in after her. After giving the driver directions to her flat, she leaned back against the buttery leather and turned her head to face Phillipe.

"Hello," he said, his voice mellow and lazy.

"Hi yourself," she replied, and smiled. "Are we crazy? We just left an exclusive party at one of the poshest hotels in Paris to hang out at my poky flat with questionable takeaway."

"Maybe a little crazy." His eyes gleamed at

her in the dark light of the car. "But that's not necessarily a bad thing. Can I tell you a secret?"

She nodded, loving the little bit of intimacy they were sharing.

"Every time I meet a celebrity, I am horribly afraid I'm going to say something stupid."

She laughed. "I don't think you're alone in that." She mused for a moment. "And you're not tongue-tied around Aurora or my—that is, the Pembertons."

"Because we have a working relationship. But tonight? Charlotte in her silk and diamonds, Stephen in his tux—which, by the way, is a lot more expensive than mine—the differences become clearer."

"Well, you're an executive manager at a multinational company known worldwide by a single name—Aurora. That still puts you miles ahead of a girl like me from Guildford, with an office administration certificate and currently unemployed."

His grin slid from his face. "Don't do that. Don't put yourself down like that. You are smart and beautiful. Do you think anyone could have organized tonight's launch like you did?" He reached for her hand. "I went through those details with you. You delegated like a champ. You oversaw the press, the guest list, worked within the budget for the event—"

"I had a massive budget," she reminded him quickly, with a quirk of her eyebrow.

He grinned. "Okay, granted. You did have a significant budget, but you did not have carte blanche and you also reconfigured the internal security at the last minute. Those are massively important skills that not everyone has." His jaw tightened. "In my opinion, you leaving is the company's loss. And the Pembertons not welcoming you in is *their* loss."

His confidence in her was a boon to her bruised ego. She reminded herself that the agreement was she'd leave with a good reference. Surely there was another company out there who could use her talents.

Phillipe wouldn't be there, though.

They whizzed through Paris, Annie looking out the window at the city she'd come to love almost as much as home. It seemed they were back to her flat in no time, and the driver was opening the door.

Phillipe got out, and then he held out his hand for her. She took it and slid out of the car, trying desperately to be graceful and not get tangled up in her long dress. With one hand in his and her other hand gripping her tiny clutch and bag of swag, she finally had both feet on the ground.

Now she had three floors to climb, and her

feet, now that she'd been off them for several minutes, were screaming at her.

"Second thoughts?" he asked, his voice soft by her ear.

She shivered. "No," she breathed. "But I'm suddenly sad that there is no elevator in my building." She held out a foot and wiggled it. The little stones glittered as she lamented the heels and the number of staircases to her floor.

Phillipe took one look at her, then lifted her into his arms and headed for the door of the building.

CHAPTER SEVEN

"PHILLIPE! PUT ME DOWN!"

He only laughed as she fumbled in her purse for keys to the door. They managed to get inside and then he headed for the stairs.

Six flights of stairs, two for each floor. He got up the first one and a half before he was regretting his impulsive gallantry.

She was giggling, though, and he liked the sound. She'd been so tense tonight, so on edge. He knew the feeling. In his heart and his head, he knew he belonged in the Aurora Inc. world. That he could fit in with the Pembertons, carry on an intelligent conversation, even be a bit witty. But it had taken him a long time to be comfortable in the setting. Annie wasn't. Maybe no one else could tell, but he could. Because he knew what one of her unfettered smiles looked like. He knew because she was treating him to one right now.

"I can't believe you picked me up. I can walk, you know."

"Your feet are killing you." He glanced down at her shoes. "Though those are some fabulous shoes."

She rotated her ankle. "Oh, you like?"

He met her gaze. "I like. I also like your arms around my neck."

"Phillipe..."

"Phillipe," he mocked, then grinned. "I am not your boss any longer. But I will put you down and keep a polite distance if that is what you wish."

He hesitated, nearly to the top of the third flight.

Her arms tightened around his neck and his pulse leaped. He'd been bracing himself for disappointment. "All right, then," he said, looking up at the three more flights. She wasn't heavy, not really, but this many stairs was a challenge.

"Am I too heavy for you?" she asked.

"Non." He kept up a steady pace. "We are nearly there."

They reached the top of the steps and he carried her to her door, then let her slide out of his arms. She was standing there, one hand holding her clutch and swag and the other fumbling with her keys, when he dipped his head and kissed her.

The bag dropped to the floor as she lifted her hands and threaded her fingers through his hair.

Mon Dieu, she was sweet. He'd been thinking about doing this for days but hadn't because of their awkward position. He would never, ever step over a line as her boss, even though the chemistry between them had been at a low simmer for weeks. It was one thing to be supportive when an employee—a friend—was struggling. It was another entirely to add a physical component to that relationship. The closest they'd gotten was the hug after she met with the family in Bella's office. Now, though… Her time at Aurora Inc. was officially over. She was in his arms and responding to his touch with such enthusiasm that it was clear his attraction was far from one-sided.

Her lips were soft, and her mouth tasted like champagne. He pulled away slightly and murmured in her ear, "Open the damned door, Anemone."

She shivered beneath his touch. "I dropped the keys," she whispered, and then gave a gasping kind of giggle that made him smile. She was so very lovely, so artless. She'd handled herself professionally earlier, but there was something about her that was less…practiced, perhaps, than the Pemberton women and, for that matter, the women he seemed to meet within this industry. She made him feel...

He reached down and picked up the keys, then slowly put them in her hand, meeting her gaze as he did so. She bit down on her bottom lip, her teeth pressing the soft flesh, and his chest cramped. She made him feel at home. It was at once a huge relief and utterly terrifying.

She spun to the door, inserting the key, while the scent of her—not Nectar, he realized—wrapped around him. A different *parfum*, with notes of jasmine, musk, cashmere. It was pretty and soft, like her.

The door opened and she stepped inside, then half turned and held the door for him to enter.

"Annie, I—"

"Kiss me again, Phillipe."

He didn't need to be asked twice. Without breaking eye contact, he slid his foot against the door and pushed it shut, then stepped forward and curled his hand around the base of her neck. She let out a sigh as his mouth came down on hers again and he stopped thinking. Now it was all about sensation—the way she moaned softly into his mouth, the vibration of the low, sexy sound, and how her body felt in his arms again. The chiffon of her dress was wispy as a fairy tale, and her skin... He ran his fingers over her shoulder and down her arm. Her skin was cool silk.

Her hands fumbled with the button of his jacket, and he moved back just a bit so she could undo it from the buttonhole. The moment it was free, she pushed it off his shoulders and she reached for his tie.

This was going to escalate very quickly if they weren't careful. His body was clearly on board with taking her to bed, but his brain wasn't quite sure. This was Annie. She didn't need one night of passion. She needed care, consideration... Love. Something he was sure he couldn't give her.

He pulled her closer for one more moment, to memorize the shape and feel of her against his body. Then he reluctantly broke the kiss, putting his hands on the smooth skin of her arms and holding her back from him just a little.

"Annie, we need to stop." She didn't answer for a moment, and when he lifted his gaze to hers, he saw confusion in her irises. "Please, don't think I don't want to, because I do. But I can't let myself be careless with you, you see?"

A tiny wrinkle formed between her brows. They were both still breathing heavily from the impassioned kisses, and it tested him sorely to hold her arms and not pull her against him again.

"Careless? Phillipe, you are the least careless man I know."

Her words reached in and touched something in his heart, something he hadn't known he needed. Perhaps because he'd been told so often that he was so focused on his studies and then his work that he failed to notice others around him—that the lack of notice was indicative of lack of caring. For Annie to see past that... Or was he making too much of her words? He gave his head a little shake.

"You are a beautiful woman, Annie. And it's not that I don't..." He ran his hand through his hair. "Having a one-night stand would be wrong. You deserve better. And I'm... I'm not able to give you more than that. So it's better if we cool off."

She stepped back, away from his hands, and smoothed her palms over her dress. "You're probably right," she agreed.

"You're also not easy to walk away from," he added, needing to be truthful, needing her to know that she was, indeed, desirable. So much so he could really use a cold shower right about now. Watching her move around the room tonight, so full of class and elegance and restrained sensuality, had sparked something in him. Something he'd ruthlessly pushed aside when she had been his employee. Without that barrier between them now... Well, it changed everything.

Her eyes shimmered for a moment, but then she blinked and they cleared. "What is it?" he asked. "Did I say something wrong?"

She shook her head. "People have been walking away from me my whole life. It's nice to know that perhaps it isn't as easy as it seems."

"Oh, Annie." Against his better judgment, he drew her into his arms again, holding her close. He felt her words so very deeply. He closed his eyes. "I know it hurts to feel... I don't know, disposable, I guess."

She nodded against his shoulder, and then pulled back and looked up. "Thank you for understanding." She gave a short laugh. "How did we go from kissing to this?"

"Because we're friends, perhaps?"

Her eyes glowed. "I like that. And it takes the sting out a little bit. Of backing away from..." Her cheeks turned an adorable shade of pink. "Well. I should stop talking."

He laughed. The truth was, it would only take a word, a touch, and he'd be on fire for her again. The sensation had washed over him so quickly the moment he'd first touched his lips to hers. She had no idea how alluring she was, how sharp the attraction running through his veins.

Kissing her had unleashed something within

him that had lain dormant for a very long time, and he was hungry for more.

"Are you still hungry?" he asked, needing to move the conversation back to something normal.

"Yes!" Her smile brightened the room. "I'm starving."

"Why don't I order in, then?"

"I'd like that." She looked down at her dress. "And I should change out of this. I would die if I got anything on it."

He was sorry to hear it; the gown was spectacular. "It is yours. You can do with it what you wish," he said, reaching for his tux jacket on the floor. He needed his phone to find a place to order from.

"Oh!" Her face flatted with alarm. "I thought it was just a loan."

Phillipe shook his head. "No, Annie. I got it for you. Having it on loan would be like saying you don't deserve to have something so beautiful, and nothing could be further from the truth. The dress, the shoes…"

"The necklace?"

He nodded.

She smiled and gave a laugh. "It's a heck of a severance package."

He laughed in response; how did she make him do that so easily? If he wasn't careful, he could fall for her. Tonight had been magical and, yes, he'd wanted that for her because he cared. It was a big step to go from there to falling in love. A step he was certain he wasn't capable of.

Unaware of the direction of his thoughts, Annie opened a few drawers and retrieved some clothes, then disappeared into the bathroom. He sat on the small sofa and scrolled through nearby takeaways, trying to ignore the path his mind was taking, envisioning her behind the closed door. "Is there anything you don't like?" he called out, looking at an online menu. Food. She'd invited him back here for food, nothing more.

"Squid and octopus!" came the automatic reply, and he grinned. Easy enough. By the time she emerged in a pair of leggings and a light sweater, he'd placed the order.

"It should be here in thirty minutes," he said, smiling up at her.

"I'm out of wine, but I have some sparkling water. Would you like a glass while we wait?" She'd taken her hair down and now tucked it behind her ear, as if somehow nervous.

"That would be nice," he replied.

"Okay. Good."

She disappeared into the tiny kitchen and came back a few minutes later with two glasses. She handed one to him and then sat next to him, tucking her legs underneath her. If she thought changing and being more casual made her any less alluring, she was dead wrong. She was pretty and soft, and the way she smiled, a little bashfully, he thought, only made him like her more.

"So, a toast," he offered, lifting his glass. "To a successful launch, and to whatever wonderful adventures are next for Anemone Jones."

"To a successful launch," she echoed. "And to moving forward for both of us."

He touched the rim of his glass to hers, then took a sip. "Moving forward for both of us? I don't think I'm going anywhere."

"Professionally I think you're set for a while," she offered. "But what you said earlier, about Madelyn...it sounds as if you're leaving some of your...resentments behind."

"Or the proverbial chip on my shoulder?"

She laughed a little. "Maybe that's a better phrase. It's hard to move past old hurts and totally understandable."

"I don't think I've moved past it, exactly." He thought back to all the ways he'd tried to make it work. He'd met Madelyn in college and had been immediately taken with her. She'd insisted that it didn't matter that she came from money and he didn't, but he'd felt the difference from the start. He'd worked to deserve her, or so he'd thought. After the wedding, he'd promised to keep her in the lifestyle she wanted, so he'd worked long hours. But the fights had started even then. He'd taken the management job, along with the prestige and the raise, to try to save their marriage. But by that time Madelyn had found someone else. When the opportunity came up to relocate to Paris, he'd jumped at it. Getting away from her had been his top priority. But perhaps he'd been lying to himself to say that the reason their marriage had failed was because of her infidelity. It wasn't so simple.

Annie took a long drink of water and then hesitated, as if pondering. "You know, I think it's okay if you don't totally move past what happened with your ex-wife. The things that hurt us most shape us. They become part of us. It wouldn't make sense for them to just disappear. The trouble comes if they keep us from moving forward."

She was very wise. "Like you finding out about your father."

She nodded. "He knew I existed. And he gave my mother money each year, and I guess that was his way of taking responsibility. But financial responsibility is the cold, bare minimum to expect from one's parent, I think. He never made an effort to know me. He didn't even want me to know his identity. And that will always sting."

"I'm so sorry," Phillipe said softly, wishing he could hold her, offer comfort. But doing so would make it far too easy to take it further. One moment he'd be touching her, holding her, and the next they'd be kissing again. The attraction still hummed between them like a tangible thing.

"How can I blame his family when he didn't even care enough to see me, even once? And what kind of person would I be if I let this one thing dictate the rest of my life?"

He had nothing to say in reply.

Annie squared her shoulders, though, and sent him a smile. "Well, I'm done now. I came here, I met them, they know I exist. Deep down I truly didn't expect them to welcome me with open arms. It's time to move on with my life."

"Here's to that," he said firmly, admiring her resolve and resilience. "Though the office is going to be remarkably dull without you there each day."

"I did like the job an awful lot," she admitted.

"Do you have any idea what is next?"

She shrugged. "I've applied to a few positions, but truthfully, Paris is expensive. It needs to be an excellent job for me to be able to afford to keep my flat."

So she really was serious about leaving Paris.

His phone buzzed and he reached for it, then glanced at the screen. "Our food is here. I'll be right back."

"I'll get plates," she offered, hopping up from the sofa.

He let himself out of the flat and went down the stairs to meet the delivery person, but he was oddly deflated.

He'd meant what he'd said about being friends. He also was insanely attracted to her. After only a few short months, and only a few weeks of really getting to know her, he realized he was going to miss her terribly when she was gone.

Anemone pressed a hand to her stomach when Phillipe left the flat, leaving the door slightly ajar for his return. Tonight had been such a whirlwind. First the transformation, then the party, which had been a lot to take in and every moment fearing she'd do something gauche or embarrassing. But more than either of those things had been kissing Phillipe, touching him, having him touch her. It had been simply splendid. It was probably foolish of her to set him on such a pedestal, but he was so smart and sexy and charming and kind. What she hadn't expected was the intensity and heat. The way he'd kicked the door shut had fired her desire so sharply she'd worried she might combust. And his reasons for backing away were totally legitimate, if disappointing.

If he hadn't, she would have gone to bed with him. Maybe it was better they didn't, and down the road perhaps she'd be thankful, but right now she was just sorry they'd stopped.

Now he was grabbing takeaway and she reminded herself to be thankful she had a friend. Even if it was only for tonight. She'd worry about tomorrow when the sun rose, and she needed to start over...again.

He came back in the flat carrying a paper bag. The scent of Chinese food hit her immediately, making her stomach growl. She carried the plates and cutlery to the small table and put them down, then went back and got the half-empty bottle of water. With a sideways grin, Phillipe unpacked the bag, setting the containers in the middle of the table. "I haven't done this in ages," he remarked, taking out two sets of chopsticks. "It's the perfect way to end the evening, I think."

She could think of one better way, but they'd agreed not to, so she topped up their glasses and handed Phillipe a paper napkin...nothing fancy here. To her surprise, he held out her chair, and then seated himself across from her. "We have noodles, and some kind of chicken, and vegetables in black bean sauce, which just happens to be a favorite of mine."

"I love spicy food, so this sounds perfect." They opened the containers and fragrant steam erupted from inside. Annie wielded her chopsticks and scooped food onto her plate. The noodles especially smelled amazing, and before long they were happily slurping noodles and munching on spicy veg and tender, gingery chicken.

"This was just what I needed," Annie said, looking over at him. He had a little sauce at the corner of his mouth, so she took her napkin and dabbed it away. "Noodles are messy, but I swear they're my favorite. I'm such a carb girl."

"I'm glad," he replied, deftly grabbing some bean sprouts in his chopsticks. "You know, normally if someone moves on at the office, we do treat them to lunch. I'm sorry we didn't arrange that for you."

"It was a hectic week and a unique situation." She looked over, feeling a little shy but determined to say what was on her mind, since she might not get another chance. "I think I prefer this, anyway. Takeaway at midnight with a handsome man wins."

Did he actually blush when she said that?

"Phillipe, about what happened before…"

She hesitated, then made herself look him in the eyes. "I liked it. I like you. I know it can't go anywhere because I'm leaving, but..." She swallowed tightly. "You should know, if things were different, I might not give up so easily."

He put down his chopsticks and took a sip of his water, then dabbed at his mouth with the napkin, all while her pulse was hammering, wondering what he was going to say.

"Annie..." He reached over and took her hand. "You tempt me."

Three words. That's all it took for her body to heat, for anticipation to ripple over her skin.

"But I can't," he said honestly. "I'm not... Well, I'm not a one-night kind of man. Call me old-fashioned, I suppose. I got carried away earlier—you're very easy to get carried away with." The hint of a smile popped his dimple just the smallest bit. "And I wouldn't hurt you for the world. That is the only reason I'm backing off. I hope you know that."

She did. He was easily the best man, the most honorable man, she'd ever met. She'd had relationships in the past—nothing ever very serious—but none of those men had taken the care with her that Phillipe had over the past two weeks.

Annie found herself rather sorry that was the case. Perhaps if she could find a way to stay in

Paris… But how? She had no savings to tide her over until she found a new job. And there was no way in hell she'd ask the Pembertons for money. They already thought she was an opportunist. Which was ironic considering she hadn't asked them for anything.

"I do know that," she assured him, pushing her plate aside. "I'm just sorry. I wish… Well, it doesn't matter. If wishes were horses and all that. But thank you. For tonight. For being a friend. For being so supportive through all of this."

"I wish I could do more. It doesn't seem fair that you're left with nothing but a reference." He frowned. "That's cold."

"It's fine," she assured him. "I don't want their money. I'm realizing now that what I wanted was something I was never going to get anyway, so it's back to reality for me. On the plus side, I worked an incredible job, got to live in Paris for the better part of a year, and I met you."

Their gazes clung for a few moments, the air filled with what she'd said and what she wasn't saying, with the knowledge of what had happened between them and what was not going to happen. She would not regret one moment of it. Not one.

"I should go," Phillipe said, clearing his throat.

He put his napkin on the table and rose. "It's getting latc."

She didn't want him to leave but he had to sometime, so she got up as well and gathered up their now-empty plates and took them to the kitchen, placing them carefully in the sink. While she was tidying, Phillipe retrieved his jacket and shrugged it on, stuffing his tie in the pocket.

She walked him to the door, feeling a little bit emptier with each step. For the past six months she'd got on well with her coworkers like Claudine and Lisette, had gone out for drinks on the odd evening, made what she considered casual friends. But none of them knew as much about her as Phillipe. None had seen past the face she showed the world to what was beneath. She was going to miss him. More than he likely realized.

"Thank you for bringing me home, and for dinner," she murmured, opening the door quietly. "It really was a great evening."

"If it was a success, it was because of you."

She chuckled and looked up at him. "We both know that's not true."

Instead of disagreeing, he stepped forward and kissed her again, a soft, simple kiss by physical standards but one that seemed to say oh-so much in the brief contact. His lips left hers, but for the smallest moment his forehead rested against hers in a gesture so tender the backs of her eyes stung.

"Please take care of yourself, Annie. And if you need anything..."

You, she thought instantly. But of course she didn't say it.

"Goodbye, Phillipe."

He nodded and left, and she shut the door behind him, half wishing he would turn around in the hallway and come back, sweep through the door and take her in his arms and say the heck with no one-night stands, let's have an unforgettable night of passion.

But that wasn't who he was, and the seconds ticked by silently until she let go of the doorknob, flicked the lock, and stepped back.

She went into the tiny kitchen and looked at the clock on the microwave. It flipped from 11:59 to twelve o'clock as she watched.

Midnight. And with the ticking of the clock, Annie knew exactly how Cinderella felt after the ball. Like she had been touched by magic and left disappointed.

CHAPTER EIGHT

THE CHIME OF her text notification woke Annie from a sound sleep. She squinted, frowned, and grappled for her phone on the tiny stand next to the bed. She was just pressing her thumb to the volume button, turning it down so she could go back to sleep, when it chimed again. And again.

Who the heck was texting her so early on a Saturday morning? Annoyed, she looked at the home screen and saw that it was already past eight…not quite as early as she'd thought.

The phone dinged again, and the message flashed on the screen.

Answer or I'm coming to Paris to find you.

Rachael. Annie flipped onto her back and unlocked the phone, shocked to see so many unread messages. What was going on?

She touched the latest message from Rachael and gave a hurried reply.

Just woke up. Give me fifteen. Don't call.

She added the last bit because she wanted to see what the fuss was about before being bombarded with questions from Rach.

There was one from Bella, just a single message, but the three short words hit Annie right in the gut, leaving her with a horrible, sinking feeling.

How could you?

What could she have possibly done? Everything last night had gone so well. And she and Phillipe had been discreet leaving together. No PDAs, nothing that would cause a fuss.

She went back to her conversation with Rachael and scrolled to the top. Once there, everything became crystal clear.

When did that secret come out?????

After the line of question marks, there was a link to a well-known gossip site. Annie held her breath as she clicked on it.

Ooh, la-la! Secret Pemberton heir at A-list party

Panic hit her right in the solar plexus as she stared at the page. There was a photo of her in that gorgeous dress, her lips smiling as she stood with Phillipe. She remembered the moment; it had been taken when Bella was making her speech. She was shoulder to shoulder with him—heavens, he was handsome. Beneath the photo was a caption.

The late Earl of Chatsworth's love child, Anemone Jones, at the Aurora Inc. launch for its new fragrance at a Paris hotel.

This was not happening. How did anyone know? How had this leaked to the press? She'd told Phillipe, no one else. The immediate family knew, but she couldn't imagine one of them would have leaked it, especially considering Bella's message this morning.

Bella's message.

She went back to her messaging app and replied quickly.

It wasn't me. I don't know who leaked it.

Of course it was highly unlikely that Bella would believe her. She wouldn't if she were in Bella's shoes. Especially since she now had nothing to lose. Her job was done. The money was gone. Of course they'd think selling her story was her ticket. And they'd think that because they didn't know her. Didn't know that she had too much integrity to do such a thing. She would rather leave Paris and start over than make money by selling a sensational story and causing her father's family harm.

Her father's family. Not hers. She needed to remember that more often, didn't she?

Her phone buzzed and she expected it was Rach again, but Phillipe's name popped up on the screen. She was fully awake now, sitting up in bed and trying to keep up with the messages and information. She clicked on his name and his message popped up.

Are you awake? I'll be there in an hour. Pack a bag.

She furrowed her brow and moved her thumbs at lightning speed.

What? Why? I'm just trying to figure out what happened.

Three dots appeared immediately: he was typing.

The news is everywhere. There will be paps at your door before you know it. I'm getting you out of Paris.

Phillipe was coming here. To whisk her out of Paris because of a scandal.

A lot of things had happened since she'd discovered Cedric Pemberton was her father, but this was by far the most surreal and jolting.

She shouldn't leave. She should stay and face her half-siblings and try to explain. She'd never been one to run away from anything. She got out of bed and went to the window, though why she walked on tiptoe, she had no idea. There were a few cars parked out front, but nothing that looked different or conspicuous. A couple sat on a bench nearby, sipping coffee, with canvas bags beside them…canvas bags, maybe big enough for a camera?

She stepped back from the window. This was ridiculous. It was one story on a gossip site. Who would be interested in her?

Apparently someone, since Bella was angry and Phillipe was concerned.

Another text came through from Phillipe.

If anyone buzzes your flat, do not answer. I'll text when I arrive. Take the back exit so you can avoid having your photo taken.

Okay, so this was clearly an overreaction. At least she thought so until her phone actually rang in her hand, startling her.

"Rachael—" she started, but her best friend cut her off.

"It's been fifteen minutes, I swear. Are you okay? Is it true? What the hell happened, and where did you get that dress?"

She really should have phoned Rachael sometime over the last few weeks, but she hadn't known where to start. "It's a long story. To sum up, the only people who knew I was Cedric Pemberton's daughter were the family, me, you, and my boss. And the doctor, I suppose, who took my DNA test."

"And you've been working at Aurora. I told you this was a mistake…"

"I know you did. It doesn't matter. I don't work there anymore. Yesterday was my last day. That was the agreement. I leave, I get a good reference. Carry on with my life."

"Hopefully with a truckload of money for your trouble."

Annie let out a slow breath, trying to get her bearings. "No money. I never wanted the money, you know that," she insisted. "And to be honest, without a job here in Paris, I was thinking of giving you a ring and seeing if I could couch surf for a few days. I thought I might come home, find a job there. Be closer to you." Her voice caught on the last bit. Rach was the only "family" she had left. In hindsight, keeping her out of the loop had been a little foolish. Rachael had every right to be mad at her, but she wasn't.

"Of course you can! But no money... Are you sure? I mean—"

"Rach, I love you, but can we table the money chat for another time? Bella has already messaged, quite upset about this being splashed on the internet. I need to figure some things out. But I promise I'll fill you in. Soon."

"Forget all that," Rachael said forcefully. "The most important thing is are you okay? Are you going to be okay today? Do you need anything? What can I do?"

"Nothing right now. I guess I'm leaving the city for a few days until this dies down. A friend is coming to pick me up in..." She glanced at her watch. "Oh, crap. In thirty minutes. I need to shower and pack a bag. I'll message when I get to where I'm going, though. Promise."

"I'm worried about you, Annie."

The concern sent warmth through Annie's chest. "I promise I'm in safe hands. You have nothing to worry about there. I'll fill you in more later, but I need to get ready."

"Message me later today to let me know you're okay."

"I will. And Rach?" Annie's throat tightened. "Thank you. For worrying. For being my friend."

"Always," Rachael answered.

They hung up and Annie darted for the shower, then pulled on a casual dress and a pair of flats. She had no idea where she was going, but she couldn't imagine it was far, so she took her carry-on bag and put in underwear, jeans, light tops, a few dresses, and a couple of pairs of shoes. It still felt like a panic over nothing, but when she went to the window again, there were more cars out front, and the people milling about definitely looked like journos.

Interested in her. What insanity. This was exactly what she'd wanted to spare the Pembertons, not that they'd ever believe her.

Her phone buzzed and she looked down.

Go out the back and turn left down the street above your building. I'm about a hundred meters down in a black Peugeot.

Surreal. Perhaps unnecessary. But the last thing she wanted to do was make things worse, so she typed back.

On my way.

She trusted Phillipe. Right now, he might be the only person she trusted.

She shouldered her bag and, at the last minute, grabbed her phone charger. Then she locked the door behind her, hurried down the stairs, and went out the back as quickly as she could before the paparazzi figured out there was a back entrance to her building to stake out.

Phillipe tapped his fingers on the steering wheel as nerves churned in his stomach. He just hoped the back exit was free from reporters and she made it to the car without being seen.

The call from William this morning had been particularly disconcerting.

The family was angry. He got that, but he also knew without a doubt that Annie hadn't contacted the press and he'd told William so. Hell, he'd been with her until nearly midnight, and she had no desire to cause any problems for the family. This had to have come from someone else, but they could think about that later. Right now he was getting her out of Paris and away from the press. That was his only concern.

A glimpse in his rearview mirror showed her hurrying toward his car. He flipped the locks and got out, reaching for her bag as she drew near. "Get in. I'll put this in the back."

She did what he said, not questioning anything. He put the bag in the back seat next to his own while she slipped into the passenger seat. He got back in and they fastened their seat belts, and then he wordlessly pulled away from the curb.

A few minutes later they had cleared the area and he let out a breath, looked over at her, and smiled. "So. Good morning."

She started to laugh, which told him she was either stressed or she appreciated the absurdity in the morning's events. He hoped it was the latter.

"Just another quiet Saturday." She shrugged, then leaned her head back against the seat. "I don't know what happened. I woke up this morning and my phone had blown up."

"I woke to a rather irate call from William," Phillipe admitted. There was no use sugar-coating anything. "The family is furious. The general consensus is that you waited until the launch to make as big a splash as possible."

"That's ridiculous! I wasn't even going to go to the launch!" Annie shook her head. "I can't imagine who could have leaked it."

"I believe you, and I told William so," Phillipe assured her. "However, the list of people who know is very small, so I understand why they automatically suspect you leaked the story even if I know it's impossible. I don't care about that. I care about you being in the line of fire from the press." He made a gesture at the interior of his car. "It was the best I could do on short notice."

Annie was silent for a few minutes as he navigated his way toward the A6. They were in for a day of driving, but he couldn't think of anywhere better to take her than home. Not because he had any burning urge to visit, though seeing his parents was long overdue, but he remembered her saying she had never been to the south of France. It was too beautiful for her to miss, and if she really meant to go back to England...

A strange emptiness filled him at the very thought. But of course she must, unless...

Unless he could help her find a reason to stay. As soon as the thought flitted through his mind, he dismissed it. To what end? As he'd told her last night, he wasn't a one-night kind of man, and he certainly wasn't interested in a relationship. His marriage crashing and burning had meant that once was enough.

He looked over at her. Her face was drawn, her lips unsmiling. As if sensing his regard, she turned her head and glanced over at him. "Where are we going?" she asked.

"Grasse," he answered. "I'm overdue to see Maman and Papa, and you did say you've never been." He tried a smile.

"Grasse? That's..." She frowned. "A long drive."

"We'll get there just before dinner," he assured her. "And I've already called ahead. Maman is making up the spare room for you and will have a lovely meal for us when we arrive."

As he said the words, he realized how unappealing it must sound. He was taking her to his family home. It was not glamorous or glitzy, just a regular home. His family was not rich. Even putting him through school had been a strain on their budget. "I'm sorry, Annie. I should have asked you first, shouldn't I? My family... Well, I grew up solidly middle class."

Her eyes flashed. "Why in the world would you apologize for that?" Her fingers twisted together. "Good heavens, Phillipe, have I given the impression that I...that is to say..." She stopped, took a breath. "Phillipe, I grew up in a very modest two-bedroom row house with a single mother who worked hard for what we had. When I look back, now I wonder how we would have made it if Cedric hadn't given Mum money. I was never hungry or cold. I had clothes to wear and went to an okay school, but there were times..." She sighed. "My flat in Paris is poky and cramped, but it suits me. Last night, with the dress and the champagne and everything... That was nice, but it's not really me. So please, don't apologize. I do not expect to be whisked away to some five-star hideaway overlooking the Mediterranean. I didn't expect to be whisked away at all. You've been a friend to me, and I appreciate that more than you know."

A friend, ha. If she knew how much time he spent reminding himself of all the reasons he shouldn't take her hand or kiss her, she'd question the friend part. And last night... Last night he would have taken her to bed, tangled with her in the sheets, listened to her soft sighs...

This was the problem. With just the slightest provocation, his mind betrayed him. It was a good thing they were staying at his parents' home. It would keep him from getting into trouble where she was concerned.

"I know you didn't do this, and I don't want to see you hounded by the press." A bubble of anger rose in his chest. "Aurora has a whole staff to deal with this kind of thing. You don't." Nor had they offered. That only added to his annoyance.

She snorted. "Phillipe, I started in the PR department, remember? I know exactly how this works."

"I suppose you do." He glanced over again as they sped along, leaving Paris behind. "Annie, we don't have to go to Grasse. I didn't ask you. I just took over the situation to get you away. I don't apologize for that, but I do apologize for acting like you had no choice in the matter. If you would like to do something else, go somewhere else, please say so."

Her face softened and she reached over and took his hand. "Grasse is fine. Staying with your family is fine, too. I'm honored." She squeezed his fingers. "But Phillipe, I'll make you a similar offer. If you would like to extricate yourself from this mess right now, there are no hard feelings. You're putting yourself in a horrible position with work."

He was. He knew it, but his sense of fairness had won out. Oh, who was he kidding... It was more than that. It was also because it was Annie. He wasn't totally sensible where she was concerned, especially after last night. She deserved better than she was getting.

"I'm owed some vacation, and the launch is done. I can take a few days." He hadn't planned to, but things changed. The company wouldn't collapse if he were absent for a day or two. "I've already emailed William about it."

And had ignored his in-box afterward. For all his glib assurances, William was going to be upset with him.

"I'm afraid I'm getting you into horrible trouble." She bit down on her lip. "Oh, what a mess."

They were still holding hands and he squeezed

hers. "Don't worry about it, Annie. All will be well. This gets you out of the line of fire for a few days so things can settle. And you'll be able to decide what *you* want to do next."

A future that didn't have him in it, he was sure. The idea niggled at him, but he didn't dwell on it. He'd made his choices, and his life was in Paris now. He'd done well for himself, proving his doubters wrong.

If he could give Annie a hand to do the same, he'd be contented with that.

No matter how much he wanted more.

Annie glanced at her phone again to check the time. It was after six; they'd stopped for lunch at a café in Lyon and went for a short walk to stretch their legs and get some air before getting back in the car for the rest of the drive. Last night she had figured she would not see Phillipe again, but today they had spent over eight hours in a car together and soon she would meet his parents.

She was a little anxious about that, actually. She hadn't really "met the parents" of the men she'd dated over the years. And even though she and Phillipe weren't dating, it still felt like a big thing. What would they think of her, the English girl running from a scandal?

Certainly, they would not think her good

enough for their son. He was so very smart, so successful.

"What's bothering you?" Phillipe asked, looking over at her.

"I'm just nervous," she answered, putting down her phone. "About meeting your parents. About all of it."

"Don't worry about that. Maman will likely have a lovely meal for us, and you will be most welcome." He smiled at her. "It's what she does. And she'll say that it has been too long since I was home."

"How long has it been?"

He went quiet for a moment, then said, "Almost two years," in a low voice.

Ah. "Since your divorce?"

"Oui."

It was interesting that the farther away from Paris they got, the more French words and phrases snuck into his sentences. She turned in her seat. "Why did you not come back, if they love you so much?" She figured she knew the answer but thought it might be good for him to admit it out loud.

"Because Madelyn is nearby, and I didn't want the reminders."

She smiled, the first genuine smile she could remember from the entire day. It felt good. "Oh, well done. I didn't think you'd admit that."

He shrugged. "It was too raw. But I've been thinking about a visit for a while. Truthfully, this situation just prompted me to make that decision a little more quickly." He smiled, too. "And I'm not sorry to have company."

"So you don't have to do it alone."

"Right again."

"Progress." She smiled at him before looking at the phone on her lap. She sighed. "So, I heard from Bella a while ago."

"Oh?" Phillipe's eyebrows rose as he glanced over, then turned to the road again.

"I told her this morning that it wasn't me. She messaged me back an hour ago saying that considering how few people knew, she didn't understand how this could have got out unless I'd either told someone or gone to the press myself. I don't know how to prove it wasn't me."

Phillipe turned on his directional and made a left-hand turn. "You shouldn't have to. I would expect they've been in meetings all day to do damage control."

"Charlotte must really be loving me right now."

Phillipe laughed. "Charlotte is distressingly good at her job. She'll come up with a way to spin this."

She sat up straighter. She was less worried about the spin and more concerned with who went to the paparazzi. Who stood to gain anything by sharing such a story? Maybe if she could figure that out, she could work her way back to who might have discovered her true identity.

She was still working through a mental list when Phillipe turned up a hillside street, slowing as he drove through a residential neighborhood. The homes here were nice—stone houses with tile roofs, olive and palm trees, little gardens. Annie had never seen a palm tree in person in her life. And here she was, in the south of France, so close to the Mediterranean. Sitting in a car with the handsomest man she'd ever known.

Was it wrong that a day that was so very horrible also kind of felt like a dream come true?

"Nous sommes ici," Phillipe said, and Annie nodded as he turned up a short drive to a welcoming-looking two-story house with wood shutters the color of whiskey barrels.

He turned off the car and let out a big breath.

"Phillipe? Before we go in, I just want to say…thank you. Thank you for caring enough to want to help me. You could have just sent me a warning, but you're a true friend."

He took off his seat belt and turned in his seat to face her better. "If I overstep, please tell me. I can be…bossy. Single-minded."

That didn't sound like the man she knew, today's activities excepted. "I will, though I won't have to. I just want you to know that I appreciate you so much. You have always—" Her throat tightened and she took a moment to swallow, ease the knot that had formed. "You have always treated me with caring and respect." She gave a small, secretive smile. "Maybe more than I wanted. You're a good man, Phillipe."

His gaze held hers and the air in the car filled with the same delicious tension that had shimmered between them last night. But then they both sat back, knowing it would only complicate matters further if they gave in to the attraction they'd done so well ignoring all day.

"Come," he said softly, giving her the smile she found so devastating. "Meet my parents. Be at home."

He retrieved their bags from the back seat and then they walked up the stone path together. Phillipe lifted his hand to knock but before he could, the door swung open and a woman stood there, her smile wide, the joy in her eyes unmistakable.

"Vous êtes ici!"

He laughed, put down the bags, and pulled her into his arms.

"Maman," he said, finally letting her go, "this is my friend, Annie."

"*Bonjour*, Annie. You are very welcome here."

The woman's English was good but heavily accented and utterly charming. "*Je suis heureuse de faire votre connaissance*, Madame Leroux. Thank you so much for having me," Annie replied, holding out her hand.

"Come in, come in! We will have dinner. Your father is in the back, grilling chicken."

"Papa? Grilling?" asked Phillipe, picking up the bags again.

"It is his new thing since he retired," she said, shaking her head. "Annie, if we forget our English, you must remind us. We do not want you to feel…left out."

"My French is getting better," Annie admitted. "Sometimes I just have a hard time keeping up."

"Come," Phillipe said. "I'll show you to your room."

He led her up the stairs to the upper level, which housed two bedrooms and a shared bathroom. "This is yours," he said, leading her to an open door. It was a sweet room, simple but welcoming, with white walls and pale blue sheer curtains that looked out over the back garden and fluttered in the breeze. A double bed and a dresser made up the only furniture in the spacious room, but there was something about it that seemed to take all the stress of the past two weeks and melt it away.

"I love it. It's so perfect."

"I'm in the other room. We'll share the bath."

"What about your parents?"

"Their bedroom is on the bottom floor. They did that a few years ago when Papa started having trouble with his knees. The doctors say he should wait a while longer for a replacement."

"This is where you grew up?"

"Yes."

She looked up at him. He'd put her bag down by the foot of the bed and suddenly everything about him seemed to fit. His workday suit was gone, and he was in jeans and a button-down, very casual and relaxed, and the lines in his face had eased even more since entering the house. "You have good memories here," she said, smiling a little. "A happy childhood."

"Yes." He looked around the room. "I shared this room with my two brothers as well. I think Maman and Papa are lonely now that none of us are local. Etienne is an engineer and lives in Dubai with his wife. Luc studied business and is with a company in Switzerland. He's married with two children. We don't see each other often."

"I didn't realize you had brothers," she said, wondering at the three of them filling up this one bedroom. How much fun they must have had. She'd always longed for a sibling…

"I am the youngest," he answered, followed by a quick smile. "And so I am the spoiled one."

"I don't believe it," she replied, and smiled back.

The moment drew out for a bit and then Phillipe stepped back. "I'll let you get settled. Meet us downstairs when you're ready. We can have a glass of wine before dinner."

She nodded, and after he was gone, she sat on the bed and texted Rachael to let her know she'd reached her destination and was safe.

Staying with a friend and their family for a few days to lie low. I'm definitely okay. I'll message soon. Xx

She went to the bathroom to freshen up a bit and when she returned Rach had messaged back. There was nothing from Bella, though. Nothing from the family at all, and that worried her. The silence was more troubling than anger.

Annie made her way downstairs and found

Phillipe and his parents out on the patio, seated at a table with a bottle of wine in the middle. She took a deep breath and then went out to meet them, putting on a smile even though she was suddenly exhausted. Phillipe rose as she approached. "You're all settled?"

"Yes, thank you." She looked at his parents. "Thank you both so much for having me."

"Papa, this is Annie. Annie, my father, Georges."

Georges smiled widely. "Phillipe, get the girl a glass of wine. Where are your manners?"

Annie laughed, instantly liking the older man. Phillipe had inherited his good looks, it seemed, in the gray-blue eyes and impish smile.

Madame Leroux gestured to the empty chair. "Please, call me Paulette. Phillipe has been telling us a little of your trouble."

"Only that you needed to get away from the press," he assured her, his eyes meeting hers as she sat. "It is your story to tell, Annie."

So he hadn't told them the details. She was glad of that. It was out anyway, but she appreciated that he had deferred that conversation until she was there. Phillipe handed her a glass of wine and she took a revivifying sip, closed her eyes, and let out a slow breath.

When she opened them, she reminded herself that she was here, in the south of France, sipping wine on a patio with friendly faces. She was safe. And oddly enough, it had been a very long time since she'd felt that way.

"My father was Cedric Pemberton," she said softly. "It is confirmed but was not public knowledge until the news broke this morning. We do not know who leaked the information, but the family thinks I sold my story. I did not. Phillipe has been a wonderful friend. He suggested getting me out of Paris to avoid the press while everything gets sorted out." She smiled over at him. "Even though it means he's in an awkward position."

"Doing what is right should never be an awkward position," he said to her, and reached over to squeeze her fingers. She longed to hold his hand, but his parents were there, and they'd promised to be only friends. The squeeze was reassuring but brief.

"It is right he brought you here. Of course you may stay as long as you like." Paulette smiled at her. "He has not been home for a visit in far too long. Maybe I should thank you for making this happen?"

"Maman..." Phillipe chided, but Annie laughed.

"Sometimes men do need a nudge before they

do what's right for them," she replied, sending Phillipe a small wink.

Paulette laughed and Georges picked up his glass. "I do not know what you are talking about."

Then everyone laughed. How was it that she could feel so at home so quickly?

Before long the grilled chicken was presented with a simple mesclun salad, some sort of flatbread and oil, and cheese. Simple and oh-so delicious. Annie let the good food and fine wine do its work, as well as the lovely, warm breeze. She could understand Phillipe loving it here. Paris was, well, Paris. But this… This was like a little slice of heaven.

She wiped her lips with her napkin and leaned back in her chair. "Last night we were at a five-star hotel with champagne and hors d'oeuvres and in our finest clothes, and I can tell you that it doesn't hold a candle to the past hour."

Paulette frowned. "Hold a candle?"

Annie smiled. "Sorry. I mean there is no comparison. This has been so very lovely. A soft spring evening with wonderful food and company is a blessing."

Georges and Phillipe shared a look, but Annie couldn't say what it meant. Just that father and son were having a silent conversation.

"Maman, Papa, Annie and I will do the washing up."

"Nonsense! It will only take a moment."

Paulette went to get up, but Phillipe put his hand on her shoulder. "If it will only take a moment, then it is no big deal."

"Yes, please," Annie said. "It is the least I can do after you made such a delicious meal."

"It was nothing," Paulette protested.

But Annie rose and put her hand on the older woman's other shoulder. "It was everything," she said softly. "You opened your home and made me feel welcome. Thank you." She swallowed around a lump in her throat. It was more than the Pembertons had shown her.

She looked up at Phillipe as they walked inside. "When we're done, I need to send an email. Do your parents have internet?"

He laughed. *"Oui,"* he answered. "How do you think we all keep in touch? Video chats."

They cleaned up the mess and then she disappeared for a few moments to charge up her laptop and to send Bella an email, saying she would be happy to share screenshots of her banking information to prove she did not receive any payments in exchange for a story. Any hopes of a relationship with her siblings had been dashed days ago. She had enough pride to want to prove her innocence, however.

They would either believe her or they wouldn't. The trip to Grasse was a way to escape the paps, but it really changed nothing. She couldn't stay here forever. At some point—soon—she'd have to carry on with her plans. And so far, couch surfing at Rachael's was the best plan she had.

CHAPTER NINE

ANNIE HADN'T EXPECTED to sleep well, but as she stretched in the strange bed, with sunlight streaming through her window, she felt incredibly rested.

There was no sound in the house at the moment, so she quietly got up and checked the time…nearly nine. She'd slept ten hours. When was the last time she'd done that? A quick check of Phillipe's room showed an open door and a made bed beyond. What a sleepyhead she was! She went back to her room and gathered up some clothes for the day, then went to have a quick shower.

She discovered Phillipe sitting in the back garden again, beneath an umbrella and sipping coffee. "Good morning," she said softly, and he looked up at her and smiled.

When he looked at her that way, she knew it didn't matter what either of them said. They would never be "just" friends.

"You slept well?"

"Better than I could have hoped. A comfy bed and a warm breeze…and maybe a full tummy and a little wine. I feel wonderful."

"You look wonderful," he said, putting down his cup. "Surprisingly relaxed, considering." He had a carafe at his elbow. "Coffee?"

"I'd love some."

He must have been anticipating her company, because another mug was on the tray with the carafe. He poured as she sat. "Where are your parents?"

"Mass," he said. "It's Sunday."

"Oh, right." She gave a little laugh. "Funny how the days suddenly started running together."

"That's not necessarily a bad thing." He handed her the cup and she took it, their fingers brushing. Tension crackled ever so briefly between them, but Annie cleared her throat and took a sip of the strong brew instead.

In the bright light of day, Annie took in the garden. The patio was made of stone and contained the gas grill, the table, chairs and umbrella, and numerous pots of plants that gave off a wonderful fragrance. There were shrubs that Annie couldn't identify, but she did recognize the showy red poppy blossoms, fragrant roses, irises, and what she thought might be valerian. "Your mother likes to garden."

"A little," he said with a nod. "More now that she and Papa have just retired. They are hoping to do some travel. And they have been volunteering at the local hospital."

"That's so lovely."

He nodded. "I had a good childhood, Annie. And their marriage…" His voice dropped off for a few moments. "Well, I wanted to have that. Clearly that's not how it worked out."

She looked at him for a long moment. There was more here than bitterness at Madelyn's affair, but she couldn't quite make out what it was. "They were your role models."

He nodded. "Sometimes I wonder if I wanted what they have so much that I ignored the signs."

"What signs?"

"That we didn't fit, I suppose. And when Madelyn became unhappy, I let my pride get in the way. I thought if I worked harder, if I could give her the life she was used to, it would be fine. But it wasn't." He sipped his coffee, stared out over the valley. "I left the job I loved thinking the promotion would make her happy. Mea culpa." Then he looked back at Annie. "You know, I thought coming back here would be painful, and yes, there are some reminders, but mostly it just feels good to be home."

"I can imagine how you feel. Guildford will always be that place for me. It's familiar, and

there were so many good times." She shifted
to look out over the small stone wall that gave
a bit of privacy. The view was stunning, down
over a valley, and she thought she might actually be able to see the sea from here. Surely not,
though… It had to just be the sky on the horizon. "I know this is home for you, but this feels
like a vacation to me. Isn't that odd?"

He smiled. "Not at all. If this is an impromptu
vacation, what would you like to do today?"

"I have no idea. I mean, coffee in the sun-
shine is a fabulous start." She laughed a little.
"What do you want to do?"

"I have an idea for tomorrow, but today… I
wondered if you'd like to go for a walk in a garden. Not just any garden, mind you."

"We're in perfume country. I wouldn't expect
it to be your average garden. I'd love to."

He smiled. "Fantastic. Let me make a call. I
know the estate owners and I'm sure we could
forgo the standard group tour for something a
little less…structured." He started to get up and
then hesitated. "But you haven't had breakfast
yet. Am I a bad host for suggesting you help
yourself to what is in the kitchen?"

"Absolutely not," she assured him. "I'm far
more comfortable with that than being waited
on. I'm sure I can find something. Am I dressed
okay?" She wasn't sure her jeans and casual top

were appropriate. Should she put on a skirt? She mentally went through her limited wardrobe choices.

"You're fine. I am going as I am." He wore gray cargo shorts and a golf shirt.

"All right."

"Let me call to be sure. But you should enjoy the patio as long as you like." He smiled. "There's still coffee in the carafe."

He disappeared into the house while she topped up her coffee. The air here was so different from Paris somehow…softer, and yes, warmer, and so fresh and fragrant. Or maybe it was just her, and how she'd needed to leave her stressful situation behind for a bit. Get out of the city. Breathe again.

Annie thought back over the past few months. She'd done nothing wrong, had she? Well, except maybe lie in the beginning…a lie of omission, but still a lie. But her motivations had all been pure. She was not going to feel guilt or anxiety over something she did not do. She had never been after financial gain, and certainly hadn't wanted to punish anyone. Even if the Pembertons didn't believe her, in her heart she knew the truth.

Energized, she picked up the coffee tray and went back inside, rummaging briefly and grabbing some fruit and a yogurt from the fridge.

Today she would not worry about Aurora or the Pembertons. Today she would walk through a garden with a gorgeous man and count her blessings.

Phillipe had always known that Anemone was sweet and lovely, but he had never imagined she'd fit in so well with his parents.

She was walking slightly ahead of him through the Mas de Pivoines gardens, her honey hair glistening in the sun. He'd once thought of her as artless, and that description remained accurate as she strolled, turning her face to the sun, stopping to take a picture with her phone as a bee lit on a flower. The tour group had started out well over an hour earlier, so Phillipe and Annie were able to meander as they pleased.

Before they'd left the house, his parents had arrived back from mass. Seeing Annie speak to them in halting French, watching his mother and father fall under her spell… It highlighted some things he had tried to ignore for years. Madelyn had never had this simple warmth about her. She wouldn't have been caught dead in faded jeans and a simple top, her hair in a ponytail for a walk in the gardens. Nor would she have looked at his backyard like it was some kind of paradise. He wasn't trying to be judgmental. He was just starting to realize that maybe the two of them hadn't quite fit together the way he'd thought they did. Was it any wonder it hadn't worked out?

Annie turned around and smiled at him. "Did you see that butterfly? So pretty." She took a deep breath and sighed. "What a glorious day. What's Paris like in the summer? I moved in October. I'm going to be sorry if I leave, aren't I? I'm going to miss Paris at the best time."

He didn't want to think about it. "Maybe you'll find a job."

"Maybe." She shrugged. "My best friend offered her couch until I find something back home. I mean, in England back home. She's in Norwich."

That was a long way. "You're really thinking of going?"

"Thinking about it." Her gaze met his. "I haven't decided anything yet. I don't want to make a big decision on impulse."

She turned back to the garden. "I love these perennial borders. It must take so much work to keep everything cared for."

"But worth it, yes?"

She nodded. "Very. And the house… It suits perfectly, too, doesn't it, with that peachy exterior and blue shutters."

He didn't answer. He simply reached for her

hand and held it as they walked along, something new and tenuous running between them.

"Phillipe…"

She turned to face him. She had sunglasses on, and she slid them up onto her head as she looked up at him. Today she wasn't wearing any makeup, and she had the smallest dusting of freckles across her nose.

"Don't say it," he said hoarsely. "Please don't. I know all the reasons. They don't stop me from wanting to kiss you."

"I was going to say thank you for bringing me here, but clearly there's more on your mind."

Oh, he was such a fool. While he tried to come up with a response, a smile bloomed on her face that put the roses to shame.

"Are you tongue-tied now?" she asked, her eyes twinkling. "I didn't think it was possible. You always seem to know what to say."

"I don't know what to say with you," he admitted finally. "Everything is at odds. And you're different here, somehow."

"So are you."

He frowned. "I am?"

She nodded. "A part of you is more relaxed, and when I see you here, it's like a lot of things just start to click together and make sense. And then there's another part of you that seems on edge."

"You are probably right on both counts." His fingers were still twined with hers. "This is my home. I have always loved it. And yet…"

She lifted her other hand and touched his face. "And yet, it's like you said this morning. Your failed marriage has ruined a bit of it for you. In coming back you accept the beauty, but it also means you have to accept the pain."

"Yes."

"And probably face some truths you would rather not face."

She was far too astute. "Maybe."

"When I go back to Paris, I have to face things. I have to face that my decisions might have been wrong. If I go back to England, I have to face that I no longer have a home to go back to. There are possessions in storage for wherever I land, but I don't know where that will be. I can ignore all that here, or at least try to. But in the back of my mind those things are always sitting there, poking me from time to time. Reality intrudes and it sucks."

He gave a small chuckle at her turn of phrase. "How do you know me so well?"

Her thumb traced along his jaw. "Sadly, I think pain recognizes pain. In some way, the people who should have loved us turned us away. It was your wife and my father, but does it really matter? Rejection is rejection. And so we learn to be strong alone."

He reached out and touched her hair, tucking an errant piece behind her ear. It was hot from the sun, fragrant from her shampoo this morning. "He was the one who lost out, Anemone."

"And she was the one who let you get away. She was a fool."

He knew he shouldn't. They kept talking about being friends and supportive. Their paths were going in different directions. But Phillipe could no more resist kissing her than a bee could resist dipping into the sweetness of a flower. He lowered his head and touched her lips with his, and this kiss was different somehow. It wasn't the champagne-induced passion of Friday night, or the temperate *this-is-goodbye* kiss when he left her flat. This was more. More of everything—awareness, gentleness, acceptance. His chest cramped from the sweetness of it.

"I kind of love it when you do that," she whispered against his lips as the kiss eased. "I know it complicates things, but I like kissing you. I could kiss you all day."

Why did she have to say things like that? It made him want to grab her hand, drag her out of the garden, take her to a hotel and spend the afternoon seducing her. He took a step backward and ran his hand through his hair. "I like it, too," he said. "Too much. Why do you think I suggested staying at my parents' instead of a hotel?"

A smile crept up her cheek. "Are you hiding behind your mother and father, Phillipe Leroux?"

He cursed—in French—and shook his head. "Of course I am. I'm trying to do the honorable thing."

She came closer again. A fragrant breeze came along and ruffled more of her hair; some had come loose as they'd been kissing. "You are definitely honorable," she agreed. "But you don't always need to be. You don't have to make that decision for me, you know. I can consent... or not."

He swallowed.

"Unless you don't want to, because you too can consent...or not."

"Annie."

She lifted up one finger. "We both know you are not ready for a relationship." She lifted a second. "We also both know that my future is up in the air and that I probably won't even be staying in the country." She lifted a third. "And I remember that you said you are not a one-night kind of guy, and I respect that. Nor am I a one-night kind of woman. Usually." She lowered her hand. "But none of those things seems able to stop what happens when we're together. I'm just saying, I'm willing to explore this during the time we have. I don't want to look back on this and have regrets either way. You don't have to protect me, Phillipe. Even though I know that sounds a bit crazy since I'm actually here because you are protecting me. But that's from the press. You don't have to protect me from being hurt or...or from myself."

God, he had such admiration for her. "You definitely know your own mind," he said, shaking his head a little in a "what am I going to do with you" kind of way. "And you're an optimist. I never quite got that until just now, but you're always looking forward, aren't you?"

She turned back to the path and started walking again, slowly. He joined her, reached for her hand again. For some reason he needed to feel connected to her in some way. Maybe for some of that optimism to rub off.

"I can't change what is behind me," she said simply. "And if I think about it too much, it gets overwhelming. So I try to live in the moment, think of the good things. And sometimes dream a little for the future. I suppose all that optimism is a little naive." They went deeper into the garden, the flowers and plants and trees affording them a privacy that felt rather intimate. "Maybe that's why my plan to work at

Aurora was flawed from the beginning. I was so sure that I could somehow sneak my way past the very obvious barrier of being a secret love child."

"Did your mother and Cedric still... I mean, after you were born."

She shook her head. "As far as I know, Cedric broke off the affair." She looked over at him. "Me coming along cost my mum the only man she ever loved. And you know, it might have saved his marriage in the end because he left her and went back to Aurora. Who knows?"

They dropped the subject for a little while, passing through an arbor where a field lay in front of them. "What is this?" she asked, staring out over the expanse.

"Lavender," he answered. "It's not the right time for it to bloom. Tomorrow I'm going to show you the most famous rose in the region. But for now, I want to show you the peonies. It's over one hundred feet of different varieties and it's splendid this time of year."

He focused on giving her the tour of the garden, including the fragrant and showy peonies that the garden was named for. Afterward, he took her to a café for a light lunch before they headed home. It seemed she was willing to let their previous conversation drop, but it kept playing in the back of his mind. What if they were to take things further? They were both consenting adults. They did not work together any longer. Neither of them was attached to anyone else. And she was right. They both knew what was standing in their way, and what this was and what it wasn't.

But there was no time to talk to her about it again, and definitely no time to act on it, as they ate another evening meal *en famille* and went to their separate beds at night.

He wondered if she was sleeping as soundly as the night before…because he surely wasn't.

He was still trying to figure out if bringing her here had been a big mistake or perhaps the smartest move he'd ever made.

For the second morning in a row, Annie woke long past sunrise and stretched, luxuriating in the soft cotton sheets of the bed.

Today Phillipe was taking her on another adventure.

Not that a walk through the gardens yesterday was really an adventure, per se, but this whole trip felt like a holiday. Grasse was stunningly beautiful. She adored the area—the undulating hills that seemed to roll right into the sea, the terraced buildings that looked like steps climbing the hillside, the warm, fragrant air. She totally understood why he said he loved it here.

It presented an additional complication, however. Because seeing him here, with his family, in the area where he'd grown up and trained... It deepened her regard for him. Her understanding of what made him tick. She was starting to care for him far too much. For all her words yesterday about being consenting adults and regrets, she knew that no matter where she ended up, having Phillipe in her life even for a short time was going to leave an indelible mark.

She wanted to hope. Clearly they liked each other, and there was no question that they were attracted to each other. But she couldn't see a way where they could get past the big things. He still maintained he did not want a relationship, and how could she blame him when he'd been hurt so badly? More than that, she was a major complication for him. His livelihood, his career, was taking off. She would not be the one to negatively affect that trajectory simply because of who she was. How could he possibly be with her and work for them? It would put him in the middle, and she refused to do that to him.

Even though she wished there might be something after this trip.

She got out of bed and tidied the sheets. If she'd learned anything over the past few years, it was that wishing never achieved anything.

But she was willing to take a risk and not play

it safe. If she had to move on, wouldn't it be nice to at least take the memory of being loved by Phillipe with her? If only he could see things the same way...

But if he did, he wouldn't be the Phillipe she'd come to know and love.

The thought stopped her hands as she was tucking the spread around the pillows. There was no *love*. She'd thought the word in a colloquial sense, that was all. A common turn of phrase: *know and love*. It didn't mean she was *in love* with him.

Though when she thought back to the tender kisses in the garden yesterday, she knew it wasn't much of a stretch. She could love him very easily. Madelyn had been a fool to cheat on him and leave him as if he meant nothing. Annie didn't know how anyone could do such a thing to a man so warm, handsome, principled. Certainly he hadn't been perfect, but still.

If he had any flaws at all, she rather thought it might be that he was too cautious. Too bound up in his sense of honor to allow himself any indulgences.

Perhaps she could convince him otherwise.

After a quick shower she dressed. Phillipe had said she should wear trousers, so she took out a pair of bone-colored linen pants, frowned at the wrinkles, and put them on anyway. She chose a pink collarless blouse to go with it, frowning again in the mirror, wondering if the ensemble was too shapeless or casual. But when she walked downstairs and into the kitchen, he turned from the counter and his eyes warmed with approval. "That is perfect. You just need a hat. Maman has said you can borrow one of hers. It will protect from the sun."

"The sun? We're going to be outdoors again?"

"*Oui*. May is the month of the rose here in Grasse. There are fields and fields of them, waiting to be plucked at just the right time to create the essential oil needed for so many perfumes. You will love it. But first, breakfast."

Paulette breezed into the kitchen from the garden. "Oh, *bien*, you are awake! I shall make fresh coffee, and the croissants are still warm."

"I feel so spoiled," Annie replied, smiling at Paulette. "The last few days have been so wonderful."

"I am enjoying it. Usually I only cook for Georges, and it is not exciting." She rolled her eyes and Annie laughed. "Phillipe says you are to go to the roses today." She got out a plate and put several croissants on it, then retrieved butter and preserves and put it all on the kitchen table. "He used to love going to the fields when he was still here in Grasse. Maybe even more than being in the lab."

"I love seeing the process from plant to perfume," he admitted. "It always feels a little bit miraculous to me."

His passion was clearly with the fragrance, so why was he stuck in an office in Paris? Why give it up? Unless it really was about the money, but he didn't strike her as the kind of man who worried about that.

Georges joined them for coffee and once they had breakfasted, they set out for the rose fields.

It took perhaps fifteen minutes for them to reach the fields. There was a large farmhouse with several outbuildings on the right, and he pulled in next to several other cars. "This is the Chabert farm. They've been growing flowers for the industry for four generations now and produce exclusively for Aurora."

"Only for you?"

"Yes." He shut off the engine and looked over at her. "I worked here as a student. When I say I started at the bottom, I really did, Annie. Roses, jasmine, lavender... This was how I fell in love with scent."

"I thought it was through chemistry."

He grinned. "I like to think of it as a marriage of science and senses. The quantifiable and the unquantifiable. Come."

They got out of the car and Phillipe led her away from the house and down over a knoll.

The scent of rose filled the air and she breathed deeply. Once they reached the field, though, she stopped and her mouth dropped open.

Rows upon rows, and workers moving among them, harvesting the blossoms as if they were ripe fruit to be plucked. "Amazing, is it not?" he asked, and she nodded, still taking it all in. "Come. Meet Andre."

She was introduced to Andre Chabert, and before long she found herself donning a white apron and putting Paulette's wide-brimmed hat on her head to keep away the sun.

"The blooms are best first thing in the morning, before the heat of the day. They cannot be wilted. Time is of the essence. I'll show you," he said, leading her to the row Andre had assigned them. In no time at all he'd shown her which blossoms were ready, how to pluck them and then tuck them into the soft apron gently to keep them from being crushed. Everyone filled their aprons and then carefully dumped the blossoms in a main bin before returning to the shrubs. She lifted her hands once and took a deep inhale of the flowers cushioned in her palms. Had anything ever smelled sweeter?

"This rose—the Centifolia rose—is so important here that there is a month-long festival happening," Phillipe explained. "It's a huge tourist draw, and we can go if you like, but I thought you'd appreciate more of a behind-the-scenes look at my city."

"This is much better than wading through crowds," she replied, invigorated by the sun, fresh air and heady scent. "I'd far rather experience it than observe."

"I thought you might." They carried on for over an hour, chatting easily, conversing in snippets with other workers who talked and laughed. Annie struggled to keep up with the French, but Phillipe translated some bits to keep her included in the conversations. As the heat from the sun grew, Phillipe drew her aside after they'd emptied their aprons once more. "I have more to show you. Would you like to see?"

She'd had such fun she could have worked all day, but the excited light in Phillipe's eyes had her nodding instantly. "Of course."

Over the course of the next few hours, Phillipe showed her how the blossoms were instantly put into burlap bags—all indelibly stamped with "Aurora"—for transport to the factory.

Then they left the Chaberts behind and he took her to the Aurora facility, where he'd plied his trade before moving to Paris.

She looked over at him as they entered not through the main doors that were there for public access, but the employee entrance. He was buzzed in and immediately a woman came around the front desk and captured him in a hug.

"Phillipe! You are home! Oh, welcome back."

Annie stood back, utterly amused, trying to imagine this sort of welcome at Aurora HQ. It simply wouldn't happen.

"*Bonjour*, Danielle. It is good to be back. I've brought a friend for a tour. I hope that is all right?"

The woman looked over at Annie and her smile widened. "Of course. Hello, I'm Danielle. I've been working this desk for fifteen years, since before Phillipe started with us in the lab."

"Annie," she replied, and held out her hand. "It's lovely to meet you."

"We've just been at Andre's. I took Annie to the morning harvest. It looks good this year."

"Things are going very well, but we miss you around here."

"I'm sure that's not true."

She wagged a finger at him. "Paris's gain is our loss. But you are here now. How long are you home for?"

"Just a few days." He didn't say more, and for that Annie was grateful. It felt a little odd being on Aurora property, if she were being honest, considering how furious the family was with her just now.

"See me before you leave again," she said as the phone rang at the desk. "Sorry. I must answer."

"Of course! *Merci*, Danielle."

He led Annie away as Danielle returned to the desk.

"She likes you a lot."

"Everyone knows each other here. It's like family."

Annie pondered that for a moment. "More so than in Paris?"

"Paris is nice, and the family has been more than welcoming. But corporate just has a different feel to it."

She nodded. "May I say something, Phillipe?"

They halted in front of a set of double doors. "Am I going to like it?" he asked.

She looked up at him. "I don't know, but I feel I must. You belong here. Seeing you at your family home, in the field, here, in this building… The pieces all seem to fit somehow. Why did you ever leave?"

A muscle tightened in his jaw. "You know why."

"Because of Madelyn?" She kept her voice low; the building wasn't exactly private.

"There were too many reminders."

"That's a shame. Because the way I see it, she not only ended your marriage, she took away something that was a part of you. Your…" She scrambled to come up with the right word. "Your essence. That's too big of a cost for any one person to pay."

He led her through the doors and into a larger room filled with what appeared to be copper tubs and pipes. "I do not dislike Paris, and I have a wonderful job," he replied.

"Not disliking something is a far cry from feeling like you are where you belong. Just think about it. Why shouldn't you be happy?"

She let the question settle and decided not to press anymore. Who was she to give life advice, anyway? Hers was in the biggest mess ever.

For the next hour, Phillipe took her on a tour of the facility, explaining the extraction process and how it took between three and five tons of rose blossoms to make a single kilo of essential oil. The sheer thought of it had her mouth dropping open, thinking of how long it had taken her to fill her apron just once this morning.

"Some of our ingredients are synthetic," he continued, taking her on a quick walk through the lab. "That's where chemistry comes in. Take, for instance, lily of the valley. It's beautiful, light, a very desirable scent, but does not produce the oil needed. So it is manufactured to mimic it instead."

She didn't know that. "There's something rather magical about having the oil from the plant, though, don't you think?"

He smiled. "I do, but I appreciate science, too. Especially when it comes to manufacturing elements we would normally source from animals."

"Ethically, I also approve." She smiled up at him.

They moved on past the mixing process and into aging. "You might think that once the oils are blended, the scent is ready, and sometimes it might be, but quite often the result is greatly improved with an aging process."

"Like wine," she offered, and he chuckled.

"Yes, I suppose. It helps the notes to all blend together. So while I blended Nectar over two years ago, it is just now ready for market as it has been aging. One must be meticulous and patient."

"And are you?" she asked, looking up at him again. "Meticulous and patient?"

Their gazes held for a few seconds, and the meaning behind her question shifted. She already knew he was patient. If he weren't, he would have taken her to bed after the launch rather than walk away. But meticulous... She swallowed, her throat tight, as she imagined being the focus of his laser-like attention.

"I try to be," he murmured, and it was as if everything around them disappeared.

The day thus far had been full of activity and new things, but one little bit of innuendo and the delicious tension between them was back. It made her breath catch and her nerve endings tingle to imagine his hands that had so gently plucked the roses this morning touching her skin.

"It's no good, is it?" he asked, his eyes searching hers.

"What isn't?"

"Avoiding this. Between us. We can pretend for a little while, but then I look at you, and I'm right back at your flat on Friday night, wanting you."

She wanted to tell him how she felt. That she was falling for him. That he was perhaps the best man she'd ever known. But that would surely send him running. He didn't want her to be in love with him. He did want her, though, and she wanted him, and it would be enough.

"I told you yesterday that we were adults, and we could consent or not. I'm consenting, Phillipe. I'm sorry you left my flat on Friday night and I've wanted to be with you ever since. I'm not going to pretend otherwise. I've been attracted to you for weeks and sometimes I feel like I might die from wanting you to touch me again."

His nostrils flared slightly as his eyes widened. "You just said that to me in the middle of a perfume factory."

"I did."

"Why the hell did I insist we stay at my parents'?"

She started to laugh, and he did, too, but then he abruptly planted a hot, searing kiss on her lips.

"Oh," she said when he released her.

"I can't offer you—"

"I'm not asking for anything. I have no idea what lies ahead, anyway. But can't we have today? I can't stay here forever, Phillipe, and neither can you. We can't run away from reality and our responsibilities indefinitely. Don't we deserve one day before we have to return to real life and deal with our messes? Or at least my mess. I dragged you into it with me."

"One day," he repeated, lifting his fingers to her cheek. "Yes, Anemone. We can have one day."

CHAPTER TEN

PHILLIPE HAD FORMED a plan in his head on the way back to the villa. If this was going to be their one chance to be together, it would not be a rushed job in his childhood bed hoping his parents didn't arrive home early from their volunteering. He was a fairly wealthy man, when all was said and done. He could afford to give her a better memory to take with her when she left.

He only felt a little guilty that he'd cut their factory tour short.

Now she was in her room, packing her bag, and he was on his phone booking a room in Cannes, which was only a half-hour drive. The first few places he tried were fully booked. But on the third he hit the jackpot: a prestige suite with a king-size bed, a soaker tub, and a balcony looking out over the water. He whipped out his credit card and booked it before he could change his mind, then took his own bag downstairs. Chances were they'd be back tomorrow, but she had been right about one thing earlier: soon they would have to deal with their responsibilities. He couldn't stay away from Paris forever. She would have to come up with a plan for moving forward as well, a plan that included what to say and what not to say to the press. Time was ticking and those decisions would have to be made soon.

But not yet.

She came downstairs as he was writing a note to his parents, explaining that he was taking Annie sightseeing for a day or two and that he would be in touch about their return. "I feel odd leaving this way," she said, standing behind him as he penned the note. "Without saying thank you."

He looked over his shoulder. "You can thank them when we return," he said, and then held his breath as he added, "unless you've changed your mind."

"I haven't," she said, coming forward. She reached a hand up into his hair and drew him down for a kiss.

She was sweet and sultry all at once and he was unnerved by the whole plan to dash away for an illicit rendezvous. It felt irresponsible somehow. The feeling wasn't strong enough to make him change his mind, however. He'd been trying to do the "right" thing for days, but as Annie said, they both knew what they wanted. Each other. There were no false hopes here. For once, Phillipe, who always seemed to plan everything with an eye to the future, was going to try living in the moment and see how it felt.

He broke the kiss and smiled against her lips. "Hold that thought," he murmured.

"For how long?"

"An hour."

She shuddered beneath his hands. "I can do an hour." He stepped back a little, and she added, "Maybe."

The drive to Cannes was blessedly short, except for one quick stop at a *pharmacie*, where he spent five minutes picking up protection for the night ahead. He was thirty-five years old, and he felt about twenty as he stood in line to pay, but he refused to be irresponsible, and it wasn't like he carried a condom all the time since he didn't do hookups. Annie had blushed when he'd pulled into the parking lot, but she hadn't said a word.

Now they were walking through the lobby of the hotel to check in, and Phillipe's body felt like a wire pulled so tight it was ready to break.

What would Annie say if she knew he had not been with a woman since his divorce?

Key card in hand, they made their way to the

elevator bank, then inside the car. He swiped the card and pushed the button for the correct floor.

The whole time his pulse hammered at his throat, his chest. The silence between them only amplified the tension, the anticipation, the *Oh-my-God-what-do-I-do-next?* feeling coursing through his veins. Out of the elevator car, down the hall, a green light on the door before he opened it and ushered them inside.

The door closed with a loud click.

Annie put down her bag; he did the same, and they stood looking at each other for a prolonged moment. Her chest rose and fell as if she'd been running, even though they'd just made the short walk from the elevator. Her cheeks were a delightful shade of pink and her eyes... Her eyes were hungry. He thrilled knowing she was hungry for him.

Then she bit down on her lip—did she not know how crazy it made him when she did that?—and began unbuttoning the pink blouse.

He had the brief thought that maybe he was supposed to be undressing, too, but he was too mesmerized by the slow play of her fingers over the covered buttons. Five, six, seven... Finally the last one was undone, and she slipped the blouse off her narrow shoulders.

She wore a blush-colored lace bra that took his breath away.

A few more moments and she had slipped out of her trousers, revealing a matching pair of bikini panties.

The last strand of his frayed restraint popped, and things moved faster after that. He pulled off his shirt and then took her in his arms, thrilling to hold her against his body, feel her skin beneath the pads of his fingers. Her kiss was equally as demanding as his, and she reached for the button of his cargo shorts, releasing it and the zipper and pushing them to the floor, taking his underwear with them. He reached for her again, sweeping her up in his arms and laying her on the bed.

She wriggled out of her panties.

"I meant to take this slow," he said, breathing heavily. "To make it good."

"We can finesse it next time," she said firmly. "Right now, I just need you, Phillipe. I need you to let go and just—" Her voice quavered with anticipation. "God. Just take me. Please."

Urgency took over. He reached into the bag for the box of condoms. In what felt like the next breath, he'd slipped inside her.

They both froze, absorbing the moment, the feeling, the ultimate connection of body to body.

Then she shifted beneath him, turned those

liquid blue eyes up to his and whispered once more, "Take me."

What else was a man supposed to do?

Annie lay on her back and stared at the ceiling, her body still humming.

She'd wanted Phillipc to let go of the polite restraint he seemed to wear like armor, and she'd thought she'd been prepared, but nothing could have prepared her for the magnificence of his lovemaking.

She started to laugh—a blissful, satisfied giggle that echoed through the suite that she hadn't even looked at yet. She was in a luxury suite on the French Riviera and all she knew was that the bed was a king and that she and Phillipe could fit on it while lying in any possible direction.

"What's so funny?"

His rich, low voice shivered over her nerve endings.

"Not funny. Happy." She paused and then added with a smile, "Satisfied."

"Mmm… Good to hear."

She let out a contented sigh.

"Just so you know, next time will be better."

She did laugh then. "If it's any better, I might combust."

"I shall make that my goal, then. To set you

on fire." He rolled to his side, and she felt his gaze on her face. "Inch by inch. Slowly."

It wouldn't take much. Just his words had her heating up all over again.

She looked over at him. "Hard and fast was what we both needed. For the first time, anyway. I've wanted to do that for weeks."

"Weeks?" His brows lifted in surprise.

"Um… Have you looked in the mirror? You're just so…*gah*! Hot, all right? And you do this thing with your eyebrow and the corner of your mouth when you smile that's so sexy. Working for you every day was sweet torture."

Said brows lifted into his hairline. "This is all news to me."

"I'm glad, because I'd have been mortified had you known."

"So the night of the party—"

"Yeah…you left me…um…" She thought of a slightly crude term normally reserved for men but said instead, "Frustrated."

He gaped at her.

She blushed.

"Well, if it's any consolation, I was feeling much the same but determined not to cross a line as your boss."

She rolled to her side and trailed her fingers over his chest. "Which I appreciate and have the utmost respect for." She smiled a little and let her hand slip over his abdomen. "And I am now ever so glad I am no longer in the employ of Aurora Inc. To think I would have missed all this…"

He laughed, a low chuckle that rumbled in his chest and filled her heart with happiness.

Thoroughly sated and in no hurry to do anything in particular, Annie finally let her gaze take in the room. It was as big as her entire studio apartment, but with much better furniture and doors leading to a balcony. "We have an ocean view, don't we?" She turned her head to study Phillipe's face. It was utterly relaxed and his eyes were closed, but he gave a small nod.

"Yes, we do."

"This place is huge. Gorgeous. It must have cost you a fortune."

He turned his head and opened one eye, squinting at her. "And worth it to have you all to myself. Though there is lots of day left if you want to explore Cannes."

She rose up on her elbow so that she was looking down into his face. Emotions she didn't want to acknowledge filled her heart and soul. He was such an easy man to love. "Cannes will always be here," she whispered, "but my time with you is short. I don't want to waste a single moment."

He opened both his eyes then, and they

burned right through to the very heart of her. This was a short-term thing; they both knew it. But it was not without connection or deep feelings for each other. She didn't want to think about it ending when it was just beginning. It would take away all the pleasure in the right now, and hadn't she earned that? She traced her finger over his cheek, along the soft curve of his lips. She'd been so lonely. Not just for the physical, though that was clearly a revelation. But the sense of having an ally. Someone to share things with, even if it was a simple meal or a glass of wine or a smile.

She appreciated him, and so she shut out the world around them and spent the next hour showing him exactly how much.

It was nearly seven when Phillipe finally insisted they dress and have dinner. Annie compromised by putting on the simple dress she'd brought with her and requesting they get room service rather than going out. "I'd like to eat on the terrace, overlooking the water with the sea breeze on my face and no one else but you."

"That sounds perfect," he agreed, so while he looked after ordering, she freshened up and then tried to make some sense of the sheets on the bed. Her cheeks flamed when she thought of how they'd spent the last several hours, but she refused to be ashamed and had no regrets. How could she when she'd felt so desired and cherished? She was self-aware enough to know she'd been starved for love for a long time, and to put what she was feeling in perspective. It didn't stop it from feeling wonderful just the same. Happiness—life, for that matter—was fleeting. It was too short to waste on regrets or perhaps even playing it safe.

She thought briefly of the Pembertons in their ivory tower and knew she wouldn't trade her life for theirs, which gave her a surprising amount of comfort. Even considering the stunning hotel room she was in now, or the glamour of the launch last week. In their world, privacy was a rare commodity and image was everything. There was so much pressure that came with the fame and fortune. As she put a swipe of gloss on her lips, she thought back to her time in the PR department. She'd come on board just after Bella had taken over as CEO and the revelation of her scars was still a news item. While she was there, she'd learned about the sabotage earlier in the spring at New York Fashion Week, which targeted Charlotte, and the scandal surrounding Stephen and Will had been all over the papers before she'd even learned that Cedric was her father.

Having her own photo show up gave her a

taste of what that was like. Fame definitely wasn't without its drawbacks. And despite everything, she did think the Pembertons were good people. All it took was putting herself in their shoes to understand their suspicions and worries.

"Dinner won't be long," Phillipe called.

She opened the bathroom door and smiled. "How do I look? Suitable for dinner *à deux*?"

"Lovely," he responded, holding out his hand. He'd changed, too, into a pair of jeans and a crisp blue shirt that brought out his eyes. "How about champagne on the deck?"

"There's champagne?"

"The ice in the bucket is mostly melted, but yes, there is champagne."

He deftly popped the cork and poured them each a glass, then they went outside to the balcony and sat at the small table and chairs.

"To running away," he offered as a toast, and she laughed and touched the rim of her glass to his before taking a drink.

Bubbles exploded over her tongue. "Rachael isn't going to believe this. Me, sitting on a balcony in Cannes, having postcoital champagne."

His eyes twinkled. "You could send her a selfie."

"I'm not eighteen."

He shrugged. "You still could." He hesitated

for a brief moment, and then said, "You do trust her, don't you?"

She nodded. "With my life."

He smiled, looking more relaxed than she'd ever seen him. "I truly don't mind if you want to message her. Friends are important. And you said she'd been very worried."

It did sound fun. And she wouldn't put in any sordid details. She popped inside to get her phone and then back out. "Here," she said, moving in close to him. He held the champagne flute in his hand as she put her head in close to his shoulder, then maneuvered her thumb to take the pic. She looked at it and got a strange swirl in her tummy. They looked so…happy. And wonderful together. She was glad he'd suggested it, because she'd have the photo now as a memory of this crazy week.

"It turned out cute," she said, and forwarded it to him.

Then she sent a copy to Rachael, prefacing it with a FYEO text.

Top secret: hiding away in Cannes with the friend I mentioned. As you can see, everything is fine.

It took less than thirty seconds for the reply to come through.

OMG you have been holding out on me! "Friend"? Right... I need details.

Annie started laughing and turned the phone to show Phillipe, who also grinned. Then she sent one last message.

About to have dinner. Just wanted you to know that I'm fine, and that I miss you. I promise to share everything soon. Xx

Then she put her phone down. She wasn't going to squander another moment of this gorgeous night with her face in a screen.

They supped on foie gras with toasted brioche, seared scallops, and roasted veal entrées, plus a bottle of a dry white that Annie was not familiar with and was most certainly out of her price range. As they ate, they talked... about their childhoods, little anecdotes about their schooling, likes and dislikes. There was laughter and a few sad moments, too, as Annie briefly mentioned losing her mother. Phillipe's strong, reassuring squeeze of her hand felt so good, so right.

"You know what bothers me the most about my father?" she asked, examining a salted caramel profiterole, wondering if she possibly had room for it after the divine meal they'd just consumed. "I thought it would be that I didn't find out until it was too late to know him. But it's not. It's knowing that he sent money. That's what's made me feel like a dirty little secret."

He nodded. "And your mother... Are you mad at her, too?"

"For not telling me? Sometimes. For getting involved with a married man who already had a family? Yes, but then I remind myself not to judge. I wasn't there. I don't know their hearts. That's the thing, though, right? I will never know their hearts, if they loved each other, if they were even happy about me."

"Annie." Phillipe scooted his chair over a little. The sunset softened the light around them, casting them in greater shadow as the sky turned pink, the same soft color as was on the rose... Heavens, had it just been this morning? It felt like a lifetime had passed between then and now.

He put his hands on hers. "I know right now that your mother was happy about you. Perhaps not at first, but from the moment you were put into her arms. How could she not be? You are wonderful. You light up every room. And as far as Cedric, well, not knowing you was his great loss. Trust me, I know this. Because right now I'm so incredibly grateful that I have had the chance to know you."

Her vision blurred as tears sprang into her eyes. "Oh, Phillipe…"

"I mean it. You have changed my life. I do not know where we go from here, but it won't be the same again, and that's a good thing." He gave a soft laugh. "I needed someone to come in and shake things up a bit."

"Oh, Phillipe, I—" She stopped abruptly, then camouflaged her near slip with a sniff. "I'm the lucky one. You could have let me be sacked and lick my wounds all the way back to Britain. Instead you fought for me. No one has ever done that for me before. And today… I'm grateful for you," she finished. And maybe inside she had said the words *I love you*—but she wouldn't ruin this beautiful evening with something that they both knew had an expiration date. It was better this way, anyway. They could go their separate ways and not have the chance for anything to be ruined.

She twined her fingers with his. "It's been a very long time since someone made me feel, I don't know, worth it, I guess. Seen and important. Losing Mum was so hard—she was my only family. And then I discovered I had another family, but I had to deal with the betrayal I felt, the loss of a parent I had never known, and fear that if my half-siblings were to discover who I was, I truly would have no one. I played it so safe, hiding who I was from them. But by doing that, I could never be a part of them, either. I was still alone. So when I say that you standing up for me is a major thing, please believe me. It means so much to me. I can never repay you for this."

"Why on earth would you have to repay anything? Maybe at first it was my sense of fairness, but I also cared about you. What would it say about me if I—"

He halted, looked away and sat back in his chair.

"What is it?" She was alarmed at how quickly he'd gone quiet, midsentence. "What's wrong?"

He turned his head and faced her again, his gaze wide with what appeared to be surprise. "Nothing is wrong, really. I just realized that I was so very quick to stand up for you, but I was never able to stand up for myself, most of all in my marriage. I've been so quick to blame Madelyn for her affair, and it was horribly wrong. There's no denying that. But the truth is we made a mistake. We never should have married in the first place. We wanted different things, even though we never really said so. Or rather, I never said so. I went along, did what I thought would make her happy, fix things, instead of being true to myself."

"Don't be too hard on yourself," she cautioned. But he shook his head. "It's not really about that. Look, I disagree with what she wanted. She wanted money and status and a certain life and I let her believe it was what I wanted, too. I mean, at least she was honest about it. I wasn't. She was off making her way as a journalist, surrounding herself with beautiful people. She thought my potential was wasted at the lab, so I put in for the management job. I left the lab behind and oversaw all the development here in Grasse. It's an enviable job, with its own prestige, but I really took it to make her happy. But she was already in another's arms by that point."

He sighed. "The funny thing was, I took that job to please her, and I thought maybe it might be a good time to talk about starting a family—the thing I wanted. But she didn't want that, either."

"Then she is the fool," Annie whispered, hating the way he was talking about himself as if he had no value. "And not worthy of you."

He gave a bitter laugh. "It's not even being worthy or not. It's that we were flawed from the beginning. I tried to prove her wrong. When the job came up in corporate, I put in for it right away. Being here—in Grasse, I mean—was just too close. So I went to Paris, and within six months I was promoted. We could have had the life she wanted. Ironic when you think about it."

"But is it the life you want?" Annie asked. "I know you said it's a great job and that Paris is 'okay,' but is it really the life you want to live? Because I've seen you the last few days, Phillipe, and you're lit up. This morning, in the fields, and then in the lab, talking about extraction and distilling and blending... That's your passion. Is Paris where you want to be, or is it here?"

He ran his hand through his hair. "I don't know anymore. But I know I have to figure it out. I've been running for two years. At some point I have to stop."

She nodded. "I want you to be happy. Everyone deserves the chance to be happy."

"And you, Annie? What do you want out of life?"

"I need to figure that out, too."

"Do you think you might be able to figure things out in Paris, at least for a while?"

The implication of his words swirled around her, as warm and seductive as the wind off the ocean. They were seated in near dark now, the sun having dipped below the horizon, with only the lights of the hotels above the beach casting their glow. Even that was muted, blocked by wide palm fronds that afforded little bits of privacy on their balcony.

He reached out and cupped her jaw. "I don't know what's next, but I don't want these few days to be the end. Can't you stay a little longer?"

She wanted to say yes. Wanted it so badly.

But she had no job, no money for rent… And she was definitely not going to ask him to support her. If they kept seeing each other, she'd feel like a kept woman. What if they decided to go their separate ways? Then she'd feel indebted. She'd rather be alone than face that kind of rejection again.

It seemed that after everything, she still had some pride left.

As she opened her mouth to answer, her phone buzzed against the table, surprising them both. Annie jumped at the jarring sound and then pressed a hand to her heart. "Oh, my. Hang on."

She lifted the phone and stared at the screen. "It's a message from Bella," she said, tapping it so she could see the entire thing. Then she looked up at Phillipe. "I've been summoned," she said, annoyance bleeding through her voice. "Apparently I'm to meet the family at the château tomorrow at noon. She is sending through the address."

"Does she say anything else?"

"No," Annie answered. "But my gut tells me that whatever happens tomorrow will determine how we all move forward."

And her gut was not giving her a good feeling.

CHAPTER ELEVEN

IT LOOKED LIKE a freaking castle.

Phillipe navigated the drive to the Pemberton château while Annie simply stared. Manicured lawns and precisely trimmed shrubs bordered the lane leading to a magnificent white structure that looked like it belonged in a fairy tale. The Aurora head office was intimidating, but this… This was a whole other level that screamed power and privilege and, she thought, home-court advantage.

"Wow," Phillipe said. "This is something."

"I might faint," Annie replied, and at least he laughed a little. She wasn't entirely joking. Walking into the boardroom with the family in attendance had been intimidating. This, on the other hand, was terrifying.

And perhaps that was exactly their intent. Annie inhaled deeply and rolled her shoulders. She would not be cowed. Not by a house. Not just any house, granted, but that didn't matter.

It was still just made of stone and glass. The people inside put their pants on one leg at a time, just like she did. She lifted her chin and kept up the internal pep talk. She would stand up for herself.

Phillipe pulled the car to a stop and reached for his seat belt, but she put her hand on his arm.

"Phillipe, I'd like to do this alone," she said quietly.

His gaze delved into hers. "Are you sure? Because I will walk in there beside you. You don't have to be alone anymore."

She melted just a bit. "I know, and I appreciate that so much. But you have already put yourself in a difficult position and I don't want to make it worse. And more than that, I need to stand up for myself. I was so naive before, and since they found out who I am I have been at the mercy of their decisions. I will not be anymore. This is the last time they will summon me anywhere. I will listen to what they have to say and then I will make my own choices." She let out a breath. "I thought I needed them. I thought I needed their acceptance to not be alone. But that's not true. I've been guided by the wrong ideas all this time, probably from grief and shock. It's time I looked at things clearly."

"All right," he said, giving a nod. "But I will

be close by. All you have to do is call and I will be back here to pick you up."

"Thank you. Wish me luck."

"I'll do better than that." He leaned over and kissed her.

Her stomach trembled with anxiety, but it was nearly noon and she needed to get this over with. Without saying anything more, she gathered her handbag and opened the car door, preparing to meet her father's family.

The door was opened by a servant before she could even reach for the knocker. "Mademoiselle Jones," he said. "If you will follow me, please."

Do not let me pass out. Do not let me pass out.

She ignored the opulence around her, knowing it would only intimidate her more. Instead she focused on her footsteps, the confident sound of her heels on the marble floor and her posture. She would walk in as an equal, she determined.

They stopped in front of a double set of doors and the servant opened them, making room for her to enter.

It was a library, and it was stunning. Floor-to-ceiling bookshelves and long windows that gave a glimpse of a garden through the wedges of light let through by the brocade draperies. And in the middle, a strategic grouping of chairs, beyond which sat a glorious fireplace that would surely crackle merrily in the winter.

The Pemberton family had taken their positions. Will and Stephen shared a settee with curved arms and tufted cushions. She was sure it was probably some Louis-whatever-number furniture—she had zero knowledge of antiques—but it looked old and expensive. Bella and Charlotte were both there as well, sitting next to each other on a set of tapestried chairs, each holding a teacup. Christophe was the only one standing, slightly behind a glorious wing chair in which Aurora was ensconced, her gray hair perfectly in place, an ice-blue suit on her slight frame. The matriarch. And, Annie was more than willing to concede, the woman who, other than herself, had been the most wronged in this whole situation. It was Aurora, therefore, who got her undivided attention.

"Lady Pemberton," she offered quietly, choosing to address her formally.

"Anemone," she offered, not unkindly, but not exactly warm, either. "Won't you please sit?" She waved her hand toward an empty chair.

"I think I'd prefer to stand for now," Annie said, trying to ignore the way her stomach twisted and knotted.

"As you wish." Aurora held eye contact.

"Thank you for coming to the château. We've found that in most cases it is more private than Paris."

"It was barely an inconvenience. I'm sure you already knew I was in Grasse." Annie saw William shift on his seat out of the corner of her eye. But Aurora was still the one who held her attention.

"We did, yes. Monsieur Leroux has been a good friend to you."

"Indeed he has, ma'am."

There was a flash of something in Aurora's eyes that Annie would almost swear was approval. Maybe faking her bravado was working just a little? But she wasn't sure how long she could sustain it.

"Miss Jones, I called for a family meeting because there are things I should say to you and my children should also hear them."

Annie was quiet and waited, forcing herself not to fidget.

And then Aurora's steely gaze softened. "I am sorry, Anemone, for the part I played in what has happened."

An apology was the last thing Anemone expected, and she could see she was not alone. A quick glance showed surprise in everyone's faces. It also seemed everyone knew now was not the time to interrupt. Annie would give Aurora this: she knew how to command a room.

"I was pregnant with Charlotte and William when I discovered Cedric's affair. It very nearly destroyed our marriage. I won't go into all the reasons why—that was between Cedric and me—but his actions afterward had very much to do with ultimatums I delivered, and they affected your life."

She paused, then leaned forward to take a drink from a glass of water sitting on the table in front of her.

"Anemone, I made Cedric promise to break off the affair. I made him promise to keep your parentage hidden, and it was I who suggested he pay your mother a biannual stipend on the condition you never know your father's identity. I wanted the whole thing to go away, and I knew your mother would struggle greatly financially. If word got out or she told you, the money would stop."

"Maman." Stephen went to her side. "Why did you...? How could you not have said something before?"

It was odd for Annie to hear emotion crackling through Stephen's voice. He was always so composed, almost to the point of being brittle. But not now. Was it possible that Aurora had kept this from all of them, even after Annie's existence had come to light?

"I was ashamed," she admitted softly.

"But…" Charlotte's voice interrupted. "But we…we've been so…" She didn't finish the sentence. Annie looked into her half-sister's face and saw remorse etched on her features.

"I know," Aurora admitted. "I am not proud of it. He did step out and have an affair, but I can't avoid my responsibility for what happened any longer." She looked up at Annie and put her hand to her heart. "Cedric agreed to all these things to save our marriage for the children we already had and the children yet to come, and he spent the rest of his life being the best husband to me. He was a good man who made some big mistakes. When he died, the money stopped. Then I heard your mother died, and that should have been the end of it."

"But she told me at the end. In her will."

"Yes, she did. And as a mother, I do not blame her for doing so. She kept her silence all those years in order to provide you with a better life."

"It paid for my schooling. We were never hungry. It might have been so very different without the money," Anemone admitted. "And I'm sorry, too, ma'am. Because my very existence must be a reminder of a very painful time in your life."

"Your existence is not as painful as knowing I was responsible for depriving you of a father and directing the course of your life."

Tears slid out of the corners of Anemone's eyes and down her cheeks. "Why now?" she asked. "You could have let this be the end and I would be gone. No more reminders."

"Because it would be wrong," she said simply. "And when things are wrong, you must do what you can to make them right."

The words settled through the room.

"I am sorry, Anemone," Aurora said softly. "Sorry for what I did and sorry I let this go on so long. I have too much pride."

"It's all right."

"You seem very forgiving."

"I got it from my mother," she said softly. "She was kind, and compassionate, and she always told me to put myself in someone else's shoes before making a judgment. It was not my fault for being born, but I also am very aware that you were the wronged woman." She lifted her chin. "But I have also tried to not sit in judgment of my mother and Cedric, either. It is not my place to judge anyone."

The room was so silent they might have heard a pin drop.

"So," Aurora continued, her shoulders relaxing a bit, "about Paris."

"Yes, that did turn out to be a bit of a mess, didn't it?" Anemone smiled faintly. "All I can say is that my decisions for moving to Paris and working at Aurora Inc. were made partly out of a misguided hope and partly out of grief. Looking back, I can see how foolish it was to try to get closer to the family in that way, and I certainly understand your mistrust of me. As far as the leak, I can only assert that I had nothing to do with that. As I told Bella—" she spared Bella a glance "—you are free to examine my banking records if that will help. I never sold my story or any part of it to the press. I went to the launch, Phillipe saw me home, and I was in bed shortly after midnight. I knew nothing until the next morning when my phone blew up, and Phillipe said he would be by to get me out of Paris for a few days while we figured out what happened. That's the whole story."

She took another breath. "My employment at Aurora is done. My plans are loose at the moment, but I am likely going to go back to England to stay with a friend while I find a new job and start over. You won't have to worry about me again."

"What about what we want?"

This came from Bella, and Annie turned a little to face the woman whose text on Saturday morning had reeked of accusation.

How could you?

"You?"

"I think I recognized from the beginning that you were not looking for leverage. You were looking for love. Does that make you naive? Very. But I recognized the look of someone needing to be loved and terrified to ask for it. I've been there enough myself, and I've always had the security of a supportive family."

Annie didn't know what to say. She scanned all the faces in the room. Charlotte looked abashed, while Stephen was looking a little shell-shocked. Will was harder to decipher, but Christophe... His face held the same softness as Bella's. Christophe had been adopted by Cedric and Aurora when his own mother hadn't been able to care for him. He knew, probably more than any of them, how she might feel.

And then her gaze lit on Aurora again.

"I think," Anemone found herself saying, "that whatever decision is made with regards to what is public knowledge about my existence must rest with Aurora. He was her husband. She is the one who will be talked about most."

Stephen spoke up. "Even if it means denying the story?"

Anemone looked at him and felt certain this was a test. Even if it weren't, she knew her answer. Maybe she was Cedric's daughter, but the only one responsible for the person she was or would become was her. She didn't need some official paternity claim to have her own identity. She was in charge of that.

"Even if it means that. Because at the end of the day, where am I? Back where I was a year ago, no better off but no worse, either. And I go on." She looked at Aurora. "Is that what you want?"

Aurora shook her head. "No."

Anemone had been fully expecting a yes, and she stood in stunned silence for a moment.

"You are Cedric Pemberton's daughter. You deserve better. I'm sorry I deprived you of that and that I also deprived you of him, because while he was not perfect, he was a loving, generous man. The PR team is at this moment polishing a draft statement acknowledging your existence and a welcome to the family."

Annie finally took the seat that she had been offered at the beginning.

Charlotte cleared her throat. "This family is no stranger to scandal. We'll weather this one, too. Take charge of the narrative. It's what we do."

It was positively shocking to hear those words from Charlotte's lips.

Bella nodded in agreement. "You can decide if you want to stay in Paris, or if you want to go back to England. The choice is yours. You are entitled to the biannual allowance that has been missed since our father's death, so you can have the freedom to make the decisions you want. It'll take a bit longer for the lawyers to work out how and if the assets of the will should be reallocated. There is a lot and it's a bit more complicated." Bella looked around at the family. "Agreed?"

"Allowance…inheritance… This isn't why I came to Paris," she said, then covered her mouth with her hand.

"You came for family." This was Christophe. "That, too, might take time. It's complicated. But for now, take what is rightfully yours. I think we all know that it is what Cedric would have wanted."

Her throat was so tight with emotion she didn't know what to say.

"He let you go to make me happy," Aurora said, her throat catching. "But he once told me that it was the hardest thing he'd ever done, walking away from his own child. Christophe is right. He would have wanted this. I should have made things right long ago, but I'm not perfect, either. I was afraid. I hope today we can all start over."

Walking away was the hardest thing he'd ever done.

Those words reached in and wrapped around her little girl's heart, the one that had thought for so long that she was so forgettable. She was fighting tears when Charlotte got up from her chair, came over and knelt before Annie. Charlotte reached out and took one of Annie's hands, opened her fingers and put the locket inside her palm. "I'm sorry, Anemone, for the part I played in this."

And that was the moment that Annie couldn't hold back the tears any longer.

Phillipe had started to get antsy the first hour after leaving Annie at the château. By the time the second hour was up, he'd started pacing outside the pub where he'd stopped and had a soft drink just to give his hands something to do. When his phone finally buzzed, two hours and twenty-six minutes after he'd driven away, he swiped across the screen to read her message.

Please join us for tea at the château.

That was it? Just "join us for tea"? He had no idea what kind of situation he was walking into.

Perhaps this was all outlining a way to eject Annie from their lives. Or some cold, calculating plan to deal with the press. Either way, she'd messaged, and he'd be there. He sent a quick response, saying he'd be there in ten minutes, and then reached inside his pocket for the car keys.

He'd had time to think during the time he'd been waiting; think about all the things Annie had said over the past few days that made perfect sense. The truth was, he did not enjoy Paris. Had he been lucky in his opportunities? Yes. Was Paris a fantastic city? Of course. But his heart was in the south, in Grasse, not in a suit in a boardroom. He'd taken that job for all the wrong reasons. And while he wasn't sure what to do now, he did know that staying in his current role wasn't what he wanted to do for the rest of his life.

He needed to go home.

And perhaps this was the best timing of all, because after today Annie would be free, wouldn't she? She wasn't locked into staying anywhere right now. They might be able to make plans...together.

Of course, it would take her a while to get past everything that had happened since her identity had been revealed. But that was fine. He would be there for her. The one thing he was absolutely sure of was that he didn't want to let her go.

For the second time that afternoon, he parked the car in the château drive and this time he got out and made his way to the front door. He rolled his shoulders and told himself to relax... He didn't need to enter like he was spoiling for a fight. He didn't generally think the Pembertons were unfair; on the contrary, he'd come to care for them a lot. But it had taken very little time for his allegiance to fall with Annie. He was already half in love with her. How could he not be? He'd never met anyone with a larger heart.

The door opened. "This way, sir," the man said, and immediately began leading him through the house.

Tea, as it happened, was being served in the gardens, which Phillipe had never seen and which, for a brief moment, made him forget his mission. They were absolutely glorious, and right now the roses were blooming profusely. An arbor with climbing roses led to a fountain, and it was there that he found the Pemberton family enjoying tea and an assortment of cakes.

How very English of them.

"Phillipe, welcome." William came forward with a smile. "Thank you for driving Anemone today." He shook Phillipe's hand. "And for getting her out of Paris to avoid the scandal. Smart move. One I've used in the past as well."

"William," he said cautiously. He still had no idea what he was walking into, though the mood seemed almost…jovial.

"You're here." Anemone was standing with a cup of tea in her hand, but she quickly put it down. "I'm sorry it took so long to text you. Let's go for a walk and I'll explain." She looked over her shoulder. "Excuse us, everyone."

So much for joining them for tea. However, if Annie wanted to fill him in, he was grateful. The last thing he wanted was to say or do the wrong thing and upset whatever fragile truce had been forged.

There was a path that led out of the garden and they headed that way, Annie's arm through his. "I have no idea where I'm going," she whispered, "but there's a path so it must be all right." She laughed a little. "This place, Phillipe. Isn't it amazing?"

He angled a look at her. "Clearly this went better than you planned. You look happy. I confess, I was expecting the worst."

"So was I." She met his gaze and he noticed what he'd missed before… There had indeed been tears. The telltale redness rimming her lashes gave it away.

She squeezed his arm. "I barely know where

to start. I guess with Aurora apologizing for forcing Cedric's hand. She told me she demanded he not see me, and that the money was to care for me but also to ensure my mother's silence."

He stopped, dumbfounded. "That's so cold."

"How would you feel if you were pregnant with twins and found out your husband had fathered another child? I can't judge her too harshly, Phillipe. Who's to say I would have done differently? Besides, there's more."

Which he expected. They'd been two hours, after all.

They walked through a stand of Aleppo pines now far enough from the house that the voices of the family were barely discernible. "And what about the rest of the family?"

"I think they realize that none of this is my fault, and I'm sure they no longer think I alerted the press. Thank you for whisking me away. I'm sure that helped. Moreover, they are immediately restoring my allowance from the estate, including what I missed over the past two years, in order that I can take some time and not worry about cash flow while making decisions."

She sounded so happy about it, but those funds were a drop in the bucket to their overall worth. Did she not understand that?

"And what do they expect in return?"

"That's just it, Phillipe. Nothing. They are not demanding my silence or anything, not like before."

"Not much point, now that the story is out."

She stopped walking and took her arm out of his. "What's wrong? I'm trying to tell you that this is all going to turn out all right and you're... I don't know what you are. You're acting like you're annoyed."

Was he? *Annoyed* wasn't the right word. *Cynical?* More than likely. "I'm just having a hard time wrapping my head around it. They haven't exactly treated you well since the news broke, Annie."

"All right. That's true. But why would I hold that against them?"

He shook his head. "Are you really that nice? Don't you ever get angry?"

She stared at him as if she didn't know him. "Phillipe, if I'm not angry at them, why are you?"

He didn't know how to answer. Maybe it was because he was tired of money and status and how it influenced people. It had certainly played a role in his divorce, and not only from Madelyn's point of view. From his. Annie was the last person he thought would be excited at the prospect of a fat deposit in her account. But maybe he didn't know her as well as he thought.

"You were so determined to not take any money before. What changed?"

She met his gaze, her eyes wide and innocent. "But before, it was to make me go away. This time, there are no conditions. Aurora said it is because it is what Cedric would have wanted, and it's the right thing to do."

"And so you automatically said yes?"

"Well, yes. Don't you see? This gives me choices, Phillipe. When I thought about going back to Paris, I had a flat I could no longer pay rent on, no job, no savings. Everything taken away except really two options—find a job immediately, which is nearly impossible, or leave France altogether and sleep on my best friend's couch. I am no longer forced into one of those scenarios."

She looked away. "That's not all, but I'm not sure I want to tell you now that I see your reaction. Which I don't understand at all, by the way."

He closed his eyes and let out a breath. He was scared. He could admit it to himself but not to anyone else. Annie was the last person on earth he'd ever thought would have her head turned by money, and he was sure that wasn't truly the case. He knew deep down she wasn't that sort of woman. At the same time, he understood why this news was so welcome. He didn't blame her for taking the money and taking some security for herself. He just was afraid that…

Afraid that if she had so many lovely options,

she wouldn't need him. And how small of a man did that make him? In his heart he wanted a happy ending for her. But right now, all he could feel was her slipping away.

Yesterday had changed everything. The words hadn't been said, but he'd never felt such an intense connection to a woman before. Being with her had made his heart soar. Hearing her laugh, seeing her with the rose blossoms in her hand, seeing the look in her eyes as she'd said, "Take me." He had left Cannes this morning a different man than yesterday.

In Cannes he had been enough. Now he wasn't so sure.

"Phillipe, I am going back to Paris tonight, and then to London for a few days. The family has decided to start looking at Cedric's will. I have no idea what the outcome will be, but they want me to have a portion of his estate."

His stomach dropped. She was about to become an heiress. Not just any heiress, but daughter of the late Earl of Chatsworth, half-sister to the current Earl…

Gone were her days of poky flats and public transit.

And then the first part of what she'd said sank in.

"You're going back to Paris? Tonight?"

She nodded, and the smile she'd been trying to keep in place slipped away completely. "I'm so sorry. I know it means you have to drive back alone, and I won't get a chance to thank your parents. But I'll be back in Paris by the weekend." She reached down and squeezed his hand. "I would love to see you and fill you in. I'm just still trying to absorb everything right now. Phillipe, I know this sounds too crazy to be true, but it's really not about the inheritance to me. It's what it represents. It's a welcome, don't you see? I might just have…a family."

He was a selfish ass. He realized that now. During their little "vacation," he'd felt as if maybe he could be her family of sorts. She'd fit in so well, with his parents, too. Would he seriously deprive her of her own family just to make himself feel better? Of course he would not.

An hour ago, he'd been thinking about asking for an actual demotion and going back to Grasse—with her. A simpler life, just the two of them. Now she was going to be a very rich woman and her entire family would be in Paris. How could he ask her to give that up when she'd just found what she'd been longing for all along?

He couldn't. He wouldn't. Instead he pulled her close and kissed her forehead. "I'm so happy for you," he murmured. "You wanted to find your family and you did. I'm not surprised. No one can stand against your sweetness for long."

Her arms snaked around his waist. "So much is going to change. I'm glad you're going to be there."

Phillipe simply held her for a few minutes, trying to cling to the memories of yesterday and wondering if their brief time together was enough to get them through what was to come.

CHAPTER TWELVE

ANNIE WAS STILL trying to wrap her head around everything that was happening.

They'd flown back to Paris in the Aurora private jet. She'd felt ridiculously conspicuous, but Christophe had taken the seat across from her, poured her a glass of wine, and before long had her laughing.

Bella wouldn't hear of Annie returning to her flat and invited her to stay at her apartment she shared with Burke. Burke was working all night at the hospital, and as Charlotte generally stayed there during her Paris trips, the three of them went to Bella's.

Charlotte was the first to break the awkward silence in the car. "Annie, I'm sorry about how I was that first day. Well, more than just the first day. We were all horrid. I was angry but I was unnecessarily cruel."

"You were hurt. I understand, Charlotte."

"You were right, though. We got to know him, and you didn't."

Annie met her half-sister's gaze. There was only a few months' difference in their ages. "I think it's okay if we say goodbye to blame. Especially blaming ourselves. It changes nothing, you know? Everyone did what they felt was best at the time, even your mother. What's important is how we move forward."

They arrived at Bella's home and before long she'd made herself at home in a guest bedroom and had joined her half-sisters—sisters!—for a cocktail. Charlotte had just called home to talk to Jacob and say good-night to their sweet baby daughter, and Bella entered the living room with a tray of cosmopolitans and a big bowl of popcorn.

They each reached for a drink, and Annie still felt a layer of awkwardness between them. "Okay, I'm just going to say it. This feels really strange."

Charlotte nodded. "Yeah, but it'll get better with time."

Bella hesitated before taking a drink. "Annie, something has been bugging me as well. I'm sorry for what I said about trusting you the morning after the launch. I knew it made no sense. If you'd wanted to sell your story, you could have done it a million times."

"Did you ever find out who leaked the news?"

"Not yet. Maybe we never will." Bella's gaze darkened. "But if it was anyone at Aurora, they'd better hope I don't find out."

"I hope it's okay if I say I'm glad." Annie shrugged and gave a small smile. "I mean, this is the end result."

They touched glasses and Annie took a sip of the vodka drink. "If you'd told me a few days ago this was where I would be, I'd have laughed."

"I know. We're really not mean people." Charlotte looked sheepish as she reached for popcorn. "It's just that when we feel threatened, we band together."

"It's how families should be," Annie said. She thought for a moment about Phillipe's parents and how she never thanked them for their hospitality. "Speaking of families, I really need to send something to Phillipe's. His parents were very welcoming."

Bella snorted into her drink. "Wait, you stayed with his parents?"

A crooked smile lifted Charlotte's cheek.

"I know, it sounds… Well, my mum would say it sounds a bit twee." She laughed. "Truly, though, I had no idea what was going on, and they have the loveliest little house. Paulette is a tremendous cook. And Phillipe did take me to the facility yesterday for a tour. I got to pick roses." She drank deeply and then realized the other two women were staring at her.

"You are totally smitten with him," Bella said.

Heat rushed up Annie's neck. "I, uh… He's been very supportive."

"Do not kid a kidder, Anemone. He fought to get your job back. He barely left your side at the launch. And at the first bit of trouble, he rode to your rescue. Even today. The moment you texted he was at the château in mere minutes. You cannot say there is nothing personal between you."

"I didn't say that," she said quietly, then looked up. "Oh, all right. I am totally smitten. He was acting strange today, though, and I'm not quite sure why." She thought back over their time together. He had asked her about staying in Paris and insinuated he wanted her there. But today when she'd told him she would be back in Paris on the weekend, he'd changed. Become very quiet. Had he changed his mind?

"It's all very new," she finally said. "Everything is new. I don't want to rush anything." Which was a lie. If Phillipe said to her this very minute that he wanted a relationship, she'd say yes. What had happened between them wasn't ordinary.

"Speaking of jobs," Charlotte said, finishing off her drink and pouring another from the pitcher, "would you be interested in staying on at Aurora? Your former job in PR hasn't been filled yct. It would give you a place to start, to learn the ropes before moving up. That is…if you even want a career with Aurora Inc."

A job. One she loved and was good at. She could keep her flat. Oh, who was she kidding. She could get a nicer flat with the other money coming her way. And she would be here, in Paris, closer to Phillipe. So they could explore what was between them.

"I would love that," she answered. "To be honest, I seriously considered never tclling you who I was because I liked the job so much and I was sure if you knew I would be out of a position. Thank you, Charlotte."

"You're welcome. You start on Monday. Your first job will be working with me on the statement to confirm your identity and your place within the Aurora empire." She smiled sweetly. "Just a minor assignment. But it can wait until you are back from London. Stephen is anxious for the two of you to meet with thc solicitors."

Oh, my.

A few more drinks were shared, and the comfort level increased. It was then that Annie asked the question that had been on her mind for months, but she had never dared ask before.

"Bella? Charlotte?"

They looked up.

"Will you tell me about Cedric?"

A smile blossomed on Bella's lips as Charlotte gave a brisk nod. "Well, here's the thing about our father. There was this one time when I was what, maybe five years old, Bel? The time that I…"

Annie held back tears as for the first time ever she was introduced to the man who'd given her life through the eyes of his other daughters. She closed her fingers around the locket. She just wished Phillipe were here with her. He was all she needed to make everything absolutely perfect.

Phillipe prepared to leave his office on Friday with the weekend stretching out before him. It had taken him all day Wednesday to drive back to Paris, and he'd been back in the office bright and early Thursday morning. It was all he knew how to do right now. His thoughts and feelings were still in such a jumble. Work was the one thing that was constant for him right now. Just too bad he couldn't seem to focus on it at all.

Well, now it was the weekend, and he'd had a text from Annie saying she would be back in

Paris today and that she'd like to see him this weekend. He hadn't yet answered because he didn't know what to say.

Tuesday morning they'd made love before leaving the hotel. They'd held hands in the car and he had thought he would be there to help her pick up the pieces after her meeting with the family.

Instead she'd been all smiles and light as the Pembertons had opened their circle to include her. And she'd jetted away on their plane without giving him another thought. Without wondering what he might be feeling.

Right now he was trying to figure out exactly who Anemone Jones really was. He knew who he wanted her to be, but—and this wasn't much of a shock—he didn't trust himself.

He'd just turned the corner out of his office when he halted, surprised to see her standing in the waiting area, in a pretty green dress and heels and a smile on her face.

"You are such a sight for sore eyes," she said, and then she came forward, moving into his embrace, holding him tightly.

He held her close because he honestly didn't know how not to; his heart had taken the lead.

"You're back."

She nodded against his collar. "This afternoon. I've been waiting for you to finish. Your office staff left twenty minutes ago." She pulled back and looked into his face. "You are happy to see me, aren't you?"

The question sent a jolt of pain through his heart, and his doubt was reflected in the concerned expression that dulled her face. "Oh." She stepped back, as if suddenly embarrassed to have hugged him. "Oh."

"I'm sorry, Annie. Yes, I'm happy to see you. I've been dying to see you since Tuesday. But there are things we need to talk about."

She nodded. "Okay. I see. Actually, no I don't. Did I do something wrong?"

Did he want to have this discussion here? Maybe. The other alternative was to go back to his place, and he hesitated to offer. He wasn't quite in the mood to put off the discussion any longer, particularly since it had been brewing for three days already.

"Not wrong. Just…" He sighed and ran his hand through his hair. "I have a lot of thoughts about what happened this week, and every one of them makes me sound like a jealous jerk. I seriously do not know how to do this."

"I can't imagine you being a jerk. You have always shown the greatest kindness and consideration. But this is eating away at you, I can tell. Let's go sit and talk about it."

She led him back into his office and to the pair of chairs set in a corner.

There was something different about her, a confidence, perhaps, that had been missing before. He liked it even though he felt it pulled her further away from him. She tucked her hair behind her ear and smiled gently, then took his hand in hers. "First of all, I need to apologize, Phillipe. So much happened on Tuesday that it wasn't until I was back in the city that night and I realized how I'd just abandoned you. I should have told the family that we would drive back the next day. It was thoughtless of me."

"But you had to go to London."

"It could have waited an extra day. I'm sorry. You went to great lengths to help me and as soon as things shifted, I was gone. Please forgive me for that."

"Of course," he murmured.

"Is that the reason you've closed yourself off to me?" she asked, her voice more hesitant. "Please, tell me what it is. It's been eating away at me. Ever since you found me in the garden at the château, something has been off. Have you changed your mind about…about us?"

His head snapped up. "Have you?"

"What?"

He ran his hand over his face. "Annie, God, I don't want to hurt you, but I have so much going on inside and I know I'm going to say it all wrong."

"Please, just say it. Not knowing and being confused is worse than having something we can talk about and deal with."

He met her gaze. "When I walked into the garden, you'd transformed. You walked in there a scared young woman with her chin held high in defiance, and the next time I saw you, you were sipping tea and telling me about a cash settlement and how you'd be flying back to Paris. It didn't fit with the Annie I had come to know. With the Annie I cared about so very much. And all I could think of was—"

He looked away.

"Was Madelyn." She finished the sentence for him, her voice barely a whisper. "Because Madelyn wanted all those things, and you did not give them to her. Am I close?"

He nodded. "I know in my head that's unfair. But my heart's been kicked a few times. It doesn't dismiss the feelings so easily."

"You must know that private jets and bags of money are not my motivators, Phillipe. At least tell me you believe that."

"I know that. I do."

She waited a full five seconds before responding. "But I left in pursuit of all those things, including meetings about a further inheritance. And I left you behind."

He nodded. "I like to think I'm a strong man, but that hit me exactly in my soft spot."

She sighed. "I need to be honest with you, too, Phillipe. There is going to be an inheritance of some sort, though it's going to take weeks or months for the legal team to figure out exactly what. In the meantime, I start my old job back here on Monday. I can get a nicer flat in a better neighborhood. Isn't that what you wanted? For me to stay in Paris so we could see where this is going? Are you trying to tell me your feelings have changed?"

"No!" The word exploded out of him, and then he tempered it with a quieter "No. That's not what I'm saying at all."

Silence fell over the office.

Finally, Annie reached out and touched his arm, prompting him to look up into her eyes. The blue depths were swimming with tears. "I'm not her," she said, a little brokenly. "I thought you knew that. I thought you got it. My head can't be turned by status and wealth."

Annie heard the words come out of her mouth and then knew exactly where everything had gone wrong. Dammit. She'd known his biggest fear and she'd unwittingly played right into it by dashing away and leaving him behind. It was more than being inconsiderate. It had been poking at his deepest wound and making it bleed again.

"Oh, Phillipe," she whispered, as a tear slid down her cheek. "I am so, so sorry. That's exactly what I did, isn't it? I was so overwhelmed with it all and the chance to be with the family that I never considered how it must look, or how you would feel."

"I did feel that way, at first. But once I thought about it, I knew you were just following what you really wanted…a family. I want you to have that, so very much."

"I was so insensitive." She slid forward, put her hands on his knees. "Phillipe, you are enough. My God, you are so much more than just enough. I hope you know that."

His chin trembled just the tiniest bit.

"I would never want to begrudge you time with your family," he said firmly. "Not when you've been searching and yearning for so long. And I do know that. Our time together forced me to look at my marriage and realize where both of us had gone wrong. Maybe Madelyn strayed, but I was trying to be something I am not. And that cannot work."

She reached out and took his hands in hers, desperately needing the connection.

He looked into her eyes. "I'm so glad you're no longer alone. And you don't need me. You're strong and resilient. Everything is going to turn out fine for you. And so you don't need me anymore."

Her mouth dropped open. "That's what you think? That I don't need you?" She shook her head, then squeezed his fingers. "Oh, Phillipe. It's not about need. You're right about that. And I never want to have to need anyone again. It sets up all sorts of obligations and expectations. *Need* is very different from *want*. And what I want for you is your happiness. I'm not sure that it's in Paris, though. I think your heart will always be in Grasse."

He slid a hand away from hers and cupped her cheek. "Darling," he said softly, "my heart is where you are. Haven't you figured out by now that I love you?"

The backs of her eyes stung. "You love me?"

He nodded. "I certainly didn't expect to. I think I knew when you walked into the ballroom that night. You looked so beautiful and yet so delightfully out of place. Our eyes met and that was it."

She sniffed. "I thought I was alone in those feelings. I really thought you'd changed your mind, that you'd decided I wasn't the one for you anymore. But love… That's different. That's not something you can just shove aside, now, is it?"

"Never," he said.

"I love you, Phillipe. In all my excitement I forgot to tell you the most important things. It wasn't the money I cared about. It was that I could now do what you wondered was possible— I could stay in Paris. I wouldn't have to go back to England and leave you behind. It would buy me time…us time…and give us a real chance. I should have said all that on Tuesday. We should have said all this on Tuesday. Instead we spent three days agonizing and speculating." She cupped his face in her hands. "I was thrilled to gain a family. But I was ecstatic that it meant I could stay close to you. That I had options for us. I knew when we were in Cannes that I loved you. Only love could have made me feel the way I did in your arms. I've never felt that way before."

He turned his head to the side and kissed the pad of the thumb cupping his cheek. "We need to communicate better," he decreed. "I've been so torn up inside."

"But being open means being vulnerable, and that's the hardest thing of all when you've been hurt. No more, though, okay? Phillipe Leroux, you are and always will be enough. Not because of your bank balance or job title or where you live, but because of the man you are. Tender, kind, funny, hardworking, passionate, honorable. Those are the reasons I love you. The only reasons that matter."

"I know you want to be with your family. And the division is looking at growth. Do you think you could be happy in Paris?"

She frowned and shook her head. "I could never ask you to stay here if you want to be somewhere else."

"It doesn't matter, as long as you're with me." He lifted her hand and kissed her knuckles. "It's different this time. I have nothing to prove. I just want you to be happy."

"I love that you'd do that for me. But I want you to know this—if you want to find a way to return home, to live and work in Grasse, I'm more than okay with it. I fell in love with it when I was there, and your parents are so wonderful. The Pembertons are amazing, and I'm happy to be a part of the family, but I still want my own life. I still want *you*, Phillipe. Whether that's in Paris or Grasse or Timbuktu."

"You mean that."

"I truly do." She leaned forward and brushed her mouth against his. "I love you."

He kissed her back and her heart soared as he murmured, "I love you, too, Annie," against her lips.

CHAPTER THIRTEEN

August

PHILLIPE LOOKED OVER at Anemone in the passenger seat and felt a wave of love wash over him. They had once again made the trip from Grasse to Provence, for a weekend with the family. It was the first real family trip with all the significant others and children—Jacob and Charlotte were bringing their daughter, and Christophe and Sophie had eight-week-old Mathieu now. Add in Will and Gabi and Bella and Burke, still newlyweds, as well as Aurora and Stephen, and it was going to be a full château.

"Happy?" he asked, as they turned up the lane and the château came into view.

"Very." She smiled over at him. "No regrets at all. Plus it'll be good to see everyone."

Good to see them because since the first of July, Phillipe and Annie had relocated to Grasse, where he was managing the department from an office at the Aurora Inc. facility.

They'd spent that weekend after her return from London at his flat, reconnecting, talking, dreaming. For the first time in his life, he'd laid everything out there: what he was passionate about, what meant the most to him, his dreams. Anemone had supported it all without hesitation. Grasse was his home. She'd already seen it for herself. They'd lain in bed and talked about possibilities and plans and it had been the scariest, most wonderful moment of his life.

Until now.

When they arrived, it was Christophe who opened the door to welcome them in. He was holding his son in his arms, and Annie immediately started to coo and fuss while Phillipe got their overnight bag.

She liked children. They'd talked about that, too.

"Phillipe, look at this little nugget! Oh, he's so sweet and he smells like baby."

"That smell can change at a moment's notice," Christophe said. "Trust me."

She carried the baby inside. Their bags were taken upstairs to their room and Christophe ushered them out to the garden, where everyone was having drinks. Phillipe was anxious but willing to be patient. After all, he'd waited a very long time for Annie. The right moment would happen.

That moment came when babies started to fuss and Charlotte and Sophie went to put them down for naps. Will and Gabi decided to take a drive into the village and Aurora went to check on dinner preparations. Stephen, ever the lone wolf, headed for the library. Everyone would reconvene for pre-dinner drinks at six.

"I'd like to stay in the garden a little longer," Annie said, breathing deeply. "It really is a bit of paradise here. And the smell! This time the lavender is blooming and it's glorious." She leaned back in her chair and closed her eyes.

Phillipe took a deep breath and reached into his pocket for the little bottle that had been resting there since their departure from home.

Then he shifted out of his chair and dropped to one knee in front of her.

"Annie," he said softly.

When she opened her eyes and saw him there, her hand flew to her mouth and tears sprang into her eyes. A smile lit him from the inside out, and he spoke around a growing lump in his throat. "Let me say all this, please."

She started to laugh; they both knew she had a thing for interrupting.

"Anemone, you gave me back myself again. You made me smile, you made me love, you made me dream. I'd forgotten how to do that, you see. But you, with your constant optimism and joy and energy… You lit a spark that had been extinguished. I will always love you for that.

"You finally found the family you were searching for, but without thinking twice you left them behind in Paris and encouraged me to follow my dreams, making them yours, too. You have loved me, and my parents, and embraced our new life with an enthusiasm that blows me away. But there is one more dream I have and today I'm asking you to share my dreams one more time by becoming my wife."

She gave a little sob-cough as he said the word *wife*, and he was horribly afraid he was going to cry himself, so he took another big breath and forced himself to carry on through the rest.

He took out the bottle, delicate pink glass with a silver band around the spherical cap. "I designed this for you," he said. "It will never go on the market. It will never be duplicated, just as you are one of a kind. The top notes are sweet and energetic, like you—pear, green apple, citrus. The heart notes… Those are the ones that are your true essence. Rose, to remind us of the day we fell in love. Jasmine, for your beauty and sensuality. And blue anemone, for you, and the excitement and anticipation I feel when I think of our lives together. And the base notes are the ones that will last long into our future. Sandalwood, for trust and unity. And vanilla, for the comfort and warmth you'll bring to our home in the years to come."

He uncapped the bottle, then took her hand in his, turned over her wrist and kissed it before adding a dab of the scent. The perfume filled the air around them with the sweetness of hopes and dreams.

He capped the bottle and put it down. When he looked at Anemone again, she was crying, happy salty tears sliding down her cheeks, and he grinned foolishly, so in love with her it was ridiculous. He reached into his pocket for the one last thing he needed to make the proposal complete. "I didn't forget a ring," he murmured, pulling out the black velvet box.

Sophie had been in on the surprise and had custom designed the ring for Phillipe. He opened the box and the diamonds sparkled in the afternoon light.

"Oh, Phillipe."

He took it out of the box and slid it on her finger. The oval diamond looked perfect, and the smaller pavé cuts made the platinum band twinkle and flash as she moved her hand.

"That's a yes, right?"

"Oh, yes! Of course I'll marry you." She got up and tugged him to his feet, then launched herself into his arms. "I can't believe you made me my own perfume."

"Of course I did," he murmured, kissing her hair, feeling like the luckiest man on earth. "Until you, I was just going through the motions. And then you came along and all my senses came alive. I love you, Anemone Jones."

"And I love you," she whispered back, before capturing him in a kiss.

When their lips finally parted, she opened her eyes and they were dancing with laughter. "Phillipe?"

"Yes, darling?"

"Let's go tell the others."

And she laughed her way out of his arms, the sound ringing through the garden like a happy benediction.

* * * * *

Look out for the next story in
Heirs to an Empire

Coming soon!

And if you enjoyed this story,
check out these other great reads from
Donna Alward

Mistletoe Kiss with the Millionaire
Wedding Reunion with the Best Man
The Heiress's Pregnancy Surprise

All available now!